CALL IT SURVIVAL

CALL IT DAMNATION

The flame shot forth, orange and cream blossoms of combustion. When they folded, Tanner sighted in the screen and squeezed the trigger. He swung the gun, and they fell. Their charred bodies lay all about him, and he added new ones to the smoldering heaps.

"Roll it!" he cried, and the car moved forward, swaying, bat bodies crunching beneath its tires.

Tanner laced the heavens with gunfire, and when they swooped again, he strafed them and fired a flare.

In the sudden magnesium glow from overhead, it seemed that millions of vampire-faced forms were circling, spiraling down toward them.

20TH CENTURY-FOX PRESENTS

DAMNATION ALLEY

JAN-MICHAEL VINCENT
GEORGE PEPPARD
DOMINIQUE SANDA
PAUL WINFIELD

JACKIE EARLE HALEY

Executive Producers
HAL LANDERS and BOBBY ROBERTS

Produced by
JEROME M. ZEITMAN and PAUL MASLANSKY

Directed by
JACK SMIGHT

Screenplay by
ALAN SHARP and LUKAS HELLER

From the novel by
ROGER ZELAZNY

Music
JERRY GOLDSMITH

A LANDERS-ROBERTS-ZEITMAN PRODUCTION

COLOR BY DeLUXE®

PANAVISION®

SOUND 360° T.M. (PATENT PENDING)

DAMNATION ALLEY

Roger Zelazny

Henry Morrison, Inc.
58 West 10th Street
New York, N. Y. 10010

SBN 425-03641-3

*BERKLEY MEDALLION BOOKS are published by
Berkley Publishing Corporation
200 Madison Avenue
New York, N. Y. 10016*

BERKLEY MEDALLION BOOK ® TM 757,375

Printed in the United States of America

Berkley Medallion Edition, NOVEMBER, 1977

SECOND PRINTING

To Del Dowling
Thanks for the way
you treated the cats

The gull swooped by, seemed to hover a moment on unmoving wings.

Hell Tanner flipped his cigar butt at it and scored a lucky hit. The bird uttered a hoarse cry and beat suddenly at the air. It climbed about fifty feet, and whether it shrieked a second time, he would never know.

It was gone.

A single white feather rocked in the violent sky, drifted out over the edge of the cliff, and descended, swinging, toward the ocean. Tanner chuckled through his beard, against the steady roar of the wind and the pounding of the surf. Then he took his feet down from the handlebars, kicked up the stand, and gunned his bike to life.

He took the slope slowly till he came to the trail, then picked up speed and was doing fifty when he hit the highway.

He leaned forward and gunned it again. He had the road all to himself, and he laid on the gas pedal till there was no place left for it to go. He raised his goggles and looked at the world through crap-colored glasses, which was pretty much the way he looked at it without them, too.

All the old irons were gone from his jacket, and he missed the swastika, the hammer and sickle, and the upright finger, especially. He missed his old emblem, too. Maybe he could pick one up in Tijuana and have some broad sew it on and . . . No. It wouldn't do. All that was dead and gone. It would be a giveaway, and he wouldn't last a day. What he *would* do was sell the Harley, work his way down the coast, clean and square, and see what he could find in the other America.

He coasted down one hill and roared up another. He tore through Laguna Beach, Capistrano Beach, San Clemente, and San Onofre. He made it down to Oceanside, where he refueled, and he passed on through Carlsbad and all those dead little beaches that fill the shore space before Solana Beach Del Mar. It was outside San Diego that they were waiting for him.

He saw the roadblock and turned. They were not sure how he had managed it that quickly, at that speed. But now he was heading away from them. He heard the gunshots and kept going. Then he heard the sirens.

He blew his horn twice in reply and leaned far forward. The Harley leaped ahead, and he wondered whether they were radioing to someone farther on up the line.

He ran for ten minutes and couldn't shake them. Then fifteen.

He topped another hill, and far ahead he saw the second block. He was bottled in.

He looked all around him for side roads, saw none.

Then he bore a straight course toward the second block. Might as well try to run it.

No good!

There were cars lined up across the entire road. They were even off the road on the shoulders.

He braked at the last possible minute, and when his speed was right he reared up on the back wheel, spun it, and headed toward his pursuers.

There were six of them coming toward him, and at his back new siren calls arose.

He braked again, pulled to the left, kicked the gas, leaped out of the seat. The bike kept going, and he hit the ground rolling, got to his feet, began running.

He heard the screeching of their tires. He heard a crash. Then there were more gunshots, and he kept going. They were aiming over his head, but he didn't know it. They wanted him alive.

After fifteen minutes he was backed against a wall of rock, and they were fanned out in front of him, and several had rifles, and they were all pointed in the wrong direction.

He dropped the tire iron he held and raised his hands.

"You got it, citizens," he said. "Take it away."

And they did.

They handcuffed him and took him back to the cars. They pushed him into the rear seat of one, and an officer got in on either side of him. Another got into the front beside the driver, and this one held a pistol in his lap.

The driver started the engine and put the car into gear, heading back up 101.

The man with the pistol turned and stared through bifocals that made his eyes look like hourglasses filled with green sand as he lowered his head. He stared for perhaps ten seconds, then said, "That was a stupid thing to do."

Hell Tanner stared back until the man said, "Very stupid, Tanner."

"Oh, I didn't know you were talking to me."

"I'm looking at you, son."

"And I'm looking at you. Hello there."

Then the driver said, without taking his eyes off the road, "You know it's too bad we've got to deliver him in good shape—after the way he smashed up the other car with that damn bike."

"He could still have an accident. Fall and crack a couple ribs, say," said the man to Tanner's left.

The man to the right didn't say anything, but the man with the pistol shook his head slowly. "Not unless he tries to escape," he said. "L.A. wants him in good shape.

"Why'd you try to skip out, buddy? You might have known we'd pick you up."

Tanner shrugged. "Why'd you pick me up? I didn't do anything."

The driver chuckled. "That's why," he said. "You didn't do anything, and there's something you were supposed to do. Remember?"

"I don't owe anybody anything. They gave me a pardon and let me go."

"You got a lousy memory, kid. You made the nation of California a promise when they turned you loose yesterday. Now you've had more than the twenty-four hours you asked for to settle your affairs. You can tell them 'no' if you want and get your pardon revoked. Nobody's forcing you. Then you can spend the rest of your life making little rocks out of big ones. We couldn't care less. I hear they got somebody else lined up already."

"Give me a cigarette," Tanner said.

The man on his right lit one and passed it to him.

He raised both hands, accepted it. As he smoked, he flicked the ashes onto the floor.

They sped along the highway, and when they went through towns or encountered traffic, the driver would hit the siren, and overhead the red light would begin winking. When this occurred, the sirens of the two other patrol cars that followed behind them would also wail. The driver never touched the brake, all the way up to L.A., and he kept radioing ahead every few minutes.

There came a sound like a sonic boom, and a cloud of dust and gravel descended upon them like hail. A tiny crack appeared in the lower-right-hand corner of the bulletproof windshield, and stones the size of marbles bounced on the hood and the roof. The tires made a crunching noise as they passed over the gravel that now lay scattered upon the road surface. The dust hung like a heavy fog, but ten seconds later they had passed out of it.

The men in the car leaned forward and stared upward.

The sky had become purple, and black lines crossed it, moving from west to east. These swelled, narrowed, moved from side to side, sometimes merged. The driver had turned on his lights by then.

"Could be a bad one coming," said the man with the pistol.

The driver nodded, and, "Looks worse farther north, too," he said.

A wailing began, high in the air above them, and the dark bands continued to widen. The sound increased in volume, lost its treble quality, became a steady roar.

The bands consolidated, and the sky grew dark as a starless, moonless night and the dust fell about them in heavy clouds. Occasionally there sounded a ping as a heavier fragment struck against the car.

The driver switched on his country lights, hit the siren again, and sped ahead. The roaring and the sound of the siren fought with one another above them, and far to the north a blue aurora began to spread, pulsing.

Tanner finished his cigarette, and the man gave him another. They were all smoking by then.

"You know, you're lucky we picked you up, boy," said the man to his left. "How'd you like to be pushing your bike through that stuff?"

"I'd like it," Tanner said.

"You're nuts."

"No. I'd make it. It wouldn't be the first time."

By the time they reached Los Angeles, the blue aurora filled half the sky, and it was tinged with pink and shot through with smoky, yellow streaks that reached like spider legs into the south. The roar was a deafening, physical thing that beat upon their eardrums and caused their skin to tingle. As they left the car and crossed the parking lot, heading toward the big, pillared building with the frieze across its forehead, they had to shout at one another in order to be heard.

"Lucky we got here when we did!" said the man with the pistol. "Step it up!" Their pace increased as they moved toward the stairway, and, "It could break any minute now!" screamed the driver.

As they had pulled into the lot, the building had the appearance of a piece of ice sculpture, with the shifting lights in the sky playing upon its surfaces and casting cold shadows. Now, though, it seemed as if it were a thing out of wax, ready to melt in an instant's flash of heat.

Their faces and the flesh of their hands took on a bloodless, corpselike appearance.

They hurried up the stairs, and a State Patrolman let them in through the small door to the right of the heavy metal double doors that were the main entrance to the building. He locked and chained the door behind them, after snapping open his holster when he saw Tanner.

"Which way?" asked the man with the pistol.

"Second floor," said the trooper, nodding

toward a stairway to their right. "Go straight back when you get to the top. It's the big office at the end of the hall."

"Thanks."

The roaring was considerably muffled, and objects achieved an appearance of natural existence once more in the artificial light of the building.

They climbed the curving stairway and moved along the corridor that led back into the building. When they reached the final office, the man with the pistol nodded to his driver. "Knock," he said.

A woman opened the door, started to say something, then stopped and nodded when she saw Tanner. She stepped aside and held the door. "This way," she said, and they moved past her into the office, and she pressed a button on her desk and told the voice that said, "Yes, Mrs. Fiske?": "They're here, with that man, sir."

"Send them in."

She led them to the dark, paneled door in the back of the room and opened it before them.

They entered, and the husky man behind the glass-topped desk leaned backward in his chair and wove his short fingers together in front of his chins and peered over them through eyes just a shade darker than the gray of his hair. His voice was soft and rasped just slightly. "Have a seat," he said to Tanner, and to the others, "Wait outside."

"You know this guy's dangerous, Mr. Denton," said the man with the pistol as Tanner seated himself in a chair situated five feet in front of the desk.

Steel shutters covered the room's three windows, and though the men could not see outside, they could guess at the possible furies that stalked there as a sound like machine-gun fire suddenly rang through the room.

"I know."

"Well, he's handcuffed, anyway. Do you want a gun?"

"I've got one."

"Okay, then. We'll be outside."

They left the room.

The two men stared at one another until the door closed, then the man called Denton said, "Are all your affairs settled now?" and the other shrugged. Then, "What the hell *is* your first name, really? Even the records show—"

"Hell," said Tanner. "That's my name. I was the seventh kid in our family, and when I was born the nurse held me up and said to my old man, 'What name do you want on the birth certificate?' and Dad said, 'Hell!' and walked away. So she put it down like that. That's what my brother told me. I never saw my old man to ask if that's how it was. He copped out the same day. Sounds right, though."

"So your mother raised all seven of you?"

"No. She croaked a couple weeks later, and different relatives took us kids."

"I see," said Denton. "You've still got a choice, you know. Do you want to try it, or don't you?"

"What's your job, anyway?" asked Tanner.

"I'm the Secretary of Traffic for the nation of California."

"What's that got to do with it?"

"I'm coordinating this thing. It could as easily have been the Surgeon General or the Postmaster General, but more of it really falls into my area of responsibility. I know the hardware best, I know the odds—"

"What are the odds?" asked Tanner.

For the first time, Denton dropped his eyes. "Well, it's risky...."

"Nobody's ever done it before, except for that nut who ran it to bring the news, and he's dead. How can you get odds out of that?"

"I know," said Denton slowly. "You're thinking it's a suicide job, and you're probably right. We're sending three cars, with two drivers in each. If any one just makes it close enough, its broadcast signals may serve to guide in a Boston driver. You don't have to go though, you know."

"I know. I'm free to spend the rest of my life in prison."

"You killed three people. You could have gotten the death penalty."

"I didn't, so why talk about it? Look, mister, I don't want to die, and I don't want the other bit either."

"Drive or don't drive. Take your choice. But remember, if you drive and you make it, all will be forgiven and you can go your own way. The nation of California will even pay for that motorcycle you appropriated and smashed up, not to mention the damage to that police car."

"Thanks a lot." And the winds boomed on the

other side of the wall and the steady staccato from the windowshields filled the room.

"You're a very good driver," said Denton after a time. "You've driven just about every vehicle there is to drive. You've even raced. Back when you were smuggling, you used to make a monthly run to Salt Lake City. There are very few drivers who'll try that, even today."

Hell Tanner smiled, remembering something.

"...And in the only legitimate job you ever held, you were the only man who'd make the mail run to Albuquerque. There've only been a few others since you were fired."

"That wasn't my fault."

"You were the best man on the Seattle run, too," Denton continued. "Your supervisor said so. What I'm trying to say is that, of anybody we could pick, you've probably got the best chance of getting through. That's why we've been indulgent with you, but we can't afford to wait any longer. It's yes or no right now, and you'll leave within the hour if it's yes."

Tanner raised his cuffed hands and gestured toward the window.

"In all this crap?" he asked.

"The car can take this storm," said Denton.

"Man, you're crazy."

"People are dying even while we're talking," said Denton.

"So a few more ain't about to make that much difference. Can't we wait till tomorrow?"

"No! A man gave his life to bring us the news!

11

And we've got to get across the continent as fast as possible now, or it won't matter! Storm or no storm, the cars leave now! Your feelings on the matter don't mean a good goddamn in the face of this! All I want out of you, Hell, is one word: Which one will it be?"

"I'd like something to eat. I haven't..."

"There's food in the car. What's your answer?"

Hell stared at the dark window.

"Okay," he said, "I'll run Damnation Alley for you. I won't leave without a piece of paper with some writing on it, though."

"I've got it here."

Denton opened a drawer and withdrew a heavy cardboard envelope, from which he extracted a piece of stationery bearing the Great Seal of the nation of California. He stood and rounded the desk and handed it to Hell Tanner.

Hell studied it for several minutes, then said, "This says that if I make it to Boston I receive a full pardon for every criminal action I've ever committed within the nation of California...."

"That's right."

"Does that include ones you might not know about now, if someone should come up with them later?"

"That's what it says, Hell—'every criminal action.'"

"Okay, you're on, fat boy. Get these bracelets off me and show me my car."

The man called Denton moved back to his seat on the other side of his desk.

"Let me tell you something else, Hell," he said. "If you try to cop out anywhere along the route, the other drivers have their orders. They will open fire on you and burn you into little bitty ashes. Get the picture?"

"I get the picture," said Hell. "I take it I'm supposed to do them the same favor?"

"That is correct."

"Good enough. That might be fun."

"I thought you'd like it."

"Now, if you'll unhook me, I'll make the scene for you."

"Not till I've told you what I think of you," Denton said.

"Okay, if you want to waste time calling me names, while people are dying—"

"Shut up! You don't care about them, and you know it! I just want to tell you that I think you are the lowest, most reprehensible human being I have ever encountered. You have killed men and raped women. You once gouged out a man's eyes, just for fun. You've been indicted twice for pushing dope, and three times as a pimp. You're a drunk and a degenerate, and I don't think you've had a bath since the day you were born. You and your hoodlums terrorized decent people when they were trying to pull their lives together after the war. You stole from them and you assaulted them, and you extorted money and the necessaries of life with the threat of physical violence. I wish you had died in the Big Raid that night, like all the rest of them. You are not a human being, except from a biological standpoint. You have a big dead spot somewhere inside you where other people have something that lets them live together in society and be neighbors. The only virtue that you possess—if you want to call it that—is that your reflexes may be a little faster, your muscles a little stronger, your eye a bit more wary than the rest of us, so that you can sit behind a wheel and drive through anything that has a way through it. It is for this that the nation of California is willing to pardon your inhumanity if you will use that one virtue to help rather than hurt. I don't approve. I don't want to depend on you, because you're not the type. I'd like to see you die in this thing, and while I hope that somebody makes it through, I hope that it will be somebody else. I hate your bloody guts. You've got your pardon now. The car's ready. Let's go."

Denton stood, at a height of about five feet, eight inches, and Tanner stood and looked down at him and chuckled.

"I'll make it," he said. "If that citizen from Boston made it through and died, I'll make it through and live. I've been as far as the Missus Hip."

"You're lying."

"No, I ain't, either, and if you ever find out that's straight, remember I got this piece of paper in my pocket—'every criminal action,' and like that. It wasn't easy, and I was lucky, too. But I made it that far, and nobody else you know can say that. So I figure that's about halfway, and I can make the other half if I can get that far."

They moved toward the door.

"I don't like to say it and mean it," said Denton, "but good luck. Not for your sake, though."

"Yeah, I know."

Denton opened the door, and, "Turn him loose," he said. "He's driving."

The officer with the pistol handed it to the man who had given Tanner the cigarettes, and he fished in his pockets for the key. When he found it, he unlocked the cuffs, stepped back, and hung them at his belt; and, "I'll come with you," said Denton. "The motor pool is downstairs."

They left the office, and Mrs. Fiske opened her purse and took a rosary into her hands and bowed her head. She prayed for Boston, and she prayed for the soul of its departed messenger. She even threw in a couple for Hell Tanner.

The bell was ringing. Its one note, relentless, interminable, filled the square. In the distance, there were other bell notes, and together they formed a demon symphony that had been going on since the dawn of time, or at least seemed as if it had.

Franklin Harbershire, President of Boston, swallowed a mouthful of cold coffee and relit his cigar. For the sixth time he picked up the fatality report, read the latest figures, threw it down again.

His desk was covered with papers covered with figures covered with ashes, and it was no good.

After seventy-six hours without sleep, nothing seemed to make sense. Least of all the attempt to quantify the death rate.

He leaned back in his leather chair, squeezed his eyes shut, and opened them again. From the inside they had been like wounds, red, swimming red.

He was aware that the figures were by now obsolete. They had also been inaccurate in the first place, for there had to be many undiscovered dead, he knew.

The bells told him that his nation was sinking slowly into the blackness that always lies a half-inch below life, waiting for the crust to weaken.

"Why don't you go home, Mr. President? Or at least take a nap? We'll watch things for you..."

He blinked his eyes and stared at the small man whose necktie had long ago vanished, along with his dark suit coat, and whose angular face now bore several days' dark growth of beard. Peabody hadn't been standing there a second ago. Had he been dozing?

He raised his cigar, to discover that it had gone out again.

"Thank you, Peabody. I couldn't sleep if I tried, though. I'm just built that way. There's nothing for me to do but wait, here."

"Well, then, would you like some fresh coffee?"

"Yes, thank you."

Peabody seemed gone for only a few seconds. Harbershire blinked his eyes, and a cup of fresh coffee was steaming beside his right hand.

"Thank you, Peabody."

"The latest figures have just come in, sir. It seems to be tapering off."

"Probably a bad sign. Fewer people to do the reporting, and fewer to handle the figures. . . . The only way we'll really know will be to take a count of the living—if there are any living—when this thing is passed, and then subtract from what we had to begin with. I don't trust these figures worth a damn."

"Neither do I, really, sir."

Harbershire burned his tongue on the coffee and drew on his cigar.

"The drivers may have made it by now, and help may be on the way."

"Possibly," said Harbershire.

"So why don't you let me get you a blanket and a pillow—and then you stretch out and get some sleep. There's nothing more to do."

"I can't sleep."

"I could find some whiskey. A couple shots might help you to relax."

"Thanks. I've had a couple."

"Even if the drivers don't make it, this thing may dry up on its own, you know."

"Maybe."

"Everybody's keeping to himself now. We've finally gotten across the idea that congregating is bad."

"That's good."

"Some people are leaving town."

"Not a bad idea. Head for the hills. May save

their necks—or some of ours, if they've got it."

He took another sip of coffee, more gingerly this time. He studied the blue smoke ladders that bent above his ashtray.

"What about the looting?" he asked.

"It's still going on. The police have killed a dozen already this evening."

"That's all we need—more deaths. Take a message to the Chief. Have the cops try to arrest them—or only wound them, if possible. Let the public think they're still shooting to kill, though."

"Yes, sir."

"I wish I could sleep. I really do, Peabody. I just can't take much more of it."

"The deaths, sir?"

"That, too."

"You mean the waiting, sir? Everyone's been admiring the way you've borne up—"

"No, not the waiting, damn it!"

He gulped more coffee and puffed a great cloud of smoke into the air.

"It's those goddamn bells," he said, gesturing at the night beyond the window. "They're driving me out of my mind!"

They descended to the basement, the subbasement and the sub-subbasement.

When they got there, Tanner saw three cars, ready to go; and he saw five men seated on benches along the wall.

One of them he recognized.

"Denny," he said, "come here," and he moved

forward, and a slim, blond youth who held a crash helmet in his right hand stood and walked toward him.

"What the hell are you doing? he asked him.

"I'm second driver in car three."

"You've got your own garage, and you've kept your nose clean. What's the thought on this?"

"Denton offered me fifty grand," said Denny, and Hell turned away his face.

"Screw it! It's no good if you're dead!"

"I need the money."

"Why?"

"I want to get married, and I can use it."

"I thought you were making out okay."

"I am, but I'd like to buy a house."

"Does your girl know what you've got in mind?"

"No."

"I didn't think so. Listen, I've got to do it—it's the only way out for me. You don't have to."

"That's for me to say."

"...So I'm going to tell you something: You drive out to Pasadena to that place where we used to play when we were kids—with the rocks and the three big trees—you know where I mean?"

"Yeah, I remember."

"Go back of the big tree in the middle, on the side where I carved my initials. Step off seven steps and dig down around four feet. Got that?"

"Yeah. What's there?"

"That's my legacy, Denny. You'll find one of those old strongboxes, probably all rusted out by now. Bust it open. It'll be full of excelsior, and there'll be a six-inch joint of pipe inside. It's threaded, and there's caps on both ends. There's a little over five grand rolled up inside it, and all the bills are clean."

"Why you telling me this?"

"Because it's yours now," he said, and hit him in the jaw.

When Denny fell, he kicked him in the ribs, three times, before the cops grabbed him and dragged him away.

"You fool!" said Denton as they held him. "You crazy, damned fool!"

"Uh-huh," said Tanner. "No brother of mine is going to run Damnation Alley while I'm around to stomp him and keep him out of the game. Better find another driver quick, because he's got cracked ribs. Or else let me drive alone."

"Then you'll drive alone," said Denton, "because we can't afford to wait around any longer. There's pills in the compartment to keep you awake, and you'd better use them, because if you fall back, they'll burn you up. Remember that."

"I won't forget you, mister, if I'm ever back in town. Don't fret about that."

"Then you'd better get into car number two and start heading up the ramp. The vehicles are all loaded. The cargo compartment is under the rear seat."

"Yeah, I know."

"... And if I ever see you again, it'll be too soon. Get out of my sight, scum!"

Tanner spat on the floor and turned his back on the Secretary of Traffic for the nation of California. Several cops were giving first aid to his brother, and one had dashed off in search of a doctor. Denton made two teams of the remaining four drivers and assigned them to cars one and three. Tanner climbed into the cab of his own, started the engine, and waited. He stared up the ramp and considered what lay ahead. He searched the compartments until he found cigarettes. He lit one and leaned back.

The other drivers moved forward and mounted their own heavily shielded vehicles. The radio crackled, crackled, hummed, crackled again, and then a voice came through as he heard the other engines come to life.

"Car one—ready!" came the voice.

There was a pause, then, "Car three—ready!" said a different voice.

Tanner lifted the microphone and mashed the button on its side.

"Car two ready," he said.

"Move out," came the order, and they headed up the ramp.

The door rolled upward before them, and they entered the storm.

It was a nightmare, getting out of L.A. and onto Route 91. The waters came down in sheets, and rocks the size of baseballs banged against the armor plating of his car. Tanner smoked and turned on the special lights. He wore infrared goggles, and the night and the storm stalked him.

The radio crackled many times, and it seemed that he heard the murmur of a distant voice, but he could never quite make out what it was trying to say.

They followed the road for as far as it went, and as their big tires sighed over the rugged terrain that began where the road ended, Tanner took the lead, and the others were content to follow. He knew the way; they didn't.

He followed the old smugglers' route he'd used to run candy to the Mormons. It was possible that he was the only one left alive that knew it. Possible; but, then, there was always someone looking for a fast buck. So, in all of L.A., there might be somebody else.

The lightning began to fall, not in bolts, but sheets. The car was insulated, but after a time his hair stood on end. He might have seen a giant Gila Monster once, but he couldn't be sure. He kept his fingers away from the fire-control board. He'd save his teeth till menaces were imminent. From the rearview scanners it seemed that one of the cars behind him had discharged a rocket, but he couldn't be sure, since he had lost all radio contact with them immediately upon leaving the building.

Waters rushed toward him, splashed about his car. The sky sounded like an artillery range. A boulder the size of a tombstone fell in front of him, and he swerved about it. Red lights flashed across the sky from north to south. In their passing, he detected many black bands going from west to east. It was not an encouraging spectacle. The storm could go on for days.

He continued to move forward, skirting a pocket of radiation that had not died in the four years since last he had come this way.

They came upon a place where the sands were fused into a glassy sea, and he slowed as he began its passage, peering ahead after the craters and chasms it contained.

Three more rockfalls assailed him before the heavens split themselves open and revealed a bright-blue light, edged with violet. The dark curtains rolled back toward the Poles, and the roaring and the gunfire reports diminished. A lavender glow remained in the north, and a green sun dipped toward the horizon at his back.

They had ridden it out, and he killed the infras, pushed back his goggles, and switched on the normal night lamps.

The desert would be bad enough, all by itself.

Something big and batlike swooped through the tunnel of his lights and was gone. He ignored its passage. Five minutes later it made a second pass, this time much closer, and he fired a magnesium flare. A black shape, perhaps forty feet across, was illuminated, and he gave it two five-second bursts from the fifty-calibers, and it fell to the ground and did not return again.

To the squares, this was Damnation Alley. To Hell Tanner, this was still the parking lot. He'd been this way thirty-two times, and so far as he was concerned, the Alley started in the place that had once been called Colorado.

He led, and they followed, and the night wore on like an abrasive.

No airplane could make it. Not since the war. None could venture above a couple hundred feet, the place where the winds began. The winds: the mighty winds that circled the globe, tearing off the tops of mountains and sequoia trees, wrecked buildings, gathering up birds, bats, insects, and anything else that moved, up into the dead belt; the winds that swirled about the world, lacing the skies with dark lines of debris, occasionally meeting, merging, clashing, dropping tons of rubbish wherever they came together and formed too great a mass. Air transportation was definitely out, to anywhere in the world. For these winds circled, and they never ceased. Not in all the twenty-five years of Tanner's memory had they let up.

Tanner pushed ahead, cutting a diagonal by the green sunset. Dust continued to fall about him, great clouds of it, and the sky was violet, then purple once more. Then the sun went down and the night came on, and the stars were very faint points of light somewhere above it all. After a time the moon rose, and the half-face that it showed that night was the color of a glass of Chianti wine held before a candle.

He lit another cigarette and began to curse, slowly, softly, and without emotion.

They threaded their way amid heaps of rubble: rock, metal, fragments of machinery, the prow of a boat. A snake, as big around as a garbage can and dark green in the cast light, slithered across Tanner's path, and he braked the vehicle as it continued and continued and continued. Perhaps a hundred-twenty feet of snake passed by before Tanner removed his foot from the brake and touched gently upon the gas pedal once again.

Glancing at the left-hand screen, which held an infrared version of the view to the left, it seemed that he saw two eyes glowing within the shadow of a heap of girders and masonry. Tanner kept one hand near the fire-control button and did not move it for a distance of several miles.

There were no windows in the vehicle, only screens which reflected views in every direction, including straight up and the ground beneath the car. Tanner sat within an illuminated box which shielded him against radiation. The "car" that he drove had eight heavily treaded tires and was thirty-two feet in length. It mounted eight fifty-caliber automatic guns and four grenade-throwers. It carried thirty armor-piercing rockets which could be discharged straight ahead or at any elevation up to forty degrees from the plane. Each of the four sides, as well as the roof of the vehicle, housed a flamethrower. Razor-sharp "wings" of tempered steel—eighteen inches wide at their bases and tapering to points, an inch and a quarter thick where they ridged—could be moved through a complete hundred-eighty-degree arc along the sides of the car and parallel to the ground, at a height of two feet and eight inches. When standing at a right angle to the body of the vehicle—eight feet to the rear of the front bumper—they extended out to a distance of six feet on either side of the car. They could be couched like lances for a charge. They could be held but slightly out from the sides for purposes of slashing whatever was sideswiped. The car was bullet-proof, air-conditioned, and had its own food locker and sanitation facilities. A long-barreled .357 Magnum was held by a clip on the door near the driver's left hand. A 30.06, a .45-caliber automatic, and six hand grenades occupied the rack immediately above the front seat.

But Tanner kept his own counsel, in the form of a long, slim SS dagger inside his right boot.

He removed his gloves and wiped his palms on the knees of his denims. The pierced heart that was tattooed on the back of his right hand was red in the light from the dashboard. The knife that went through it was dark blue, and his first name was tattooed in the same color beneath it, one letter on each knuckle, beginning with that at the base of his little finger.

He opened and explored the two near compartments but could find no cigars. So he crushed out his cigarette on the floor and lit another.

The forward screen showed vegetation, and he slowed. He tried using the radio but couldn't tell whether anyone heard him, receiving only static in reply.

He stared ahead and up. He halted once again.

He turned his forward lights up to full intensity and studied the situation.

A heavy wall of thorn bushes stood before him, reaching to a height of perhaps twelve feet. It swept on to his right and off to his left, vanishing out of sight in both directions. How dense, how deep it might be, he could not tell. It had not been there a few years before.

He moved forward slowly and activated the flamethrowers. In the rearview screen, he could see that the other vehicles had halted a hundred yards behind him and dimmed their lights.

He drove till he could go no farther, then pressed the button for the forward flame.

It shot forth, a tongue of fire, licking fifty feet into the bramble. He held it for five seconds and withdrew it. Then he extended it a second time and backed away quickly as the flames caught.

Beginning with a tiny glow they worked their way upward and spread slowly to the right and the left. Then they grew in size and brightness.

As Tanner backed away, he had to dim his screen, for they'd spread fifty feet before he'd backed more than a hundred, and they leaped thirty and forty feet into the air.

The blaze widened, to a hundred feet, two, three … As Tanner backed away, he could see a river of fire flowing off into the distance, and the night was bright about him.

He watched it burn, until it seemed that he looked upon a molten sea. Then he searched the refrigerator, but there was no beer. He opened a soft drink and sipped it while he watched the burning. After about ten minutes the air-conditioner whined and shook itself to life. Hordes of dark, four-footed creatures, the size of rats or cats, fled from the inferno, their coats smoldering. They flowed by. At one point they covered his forward screen, and he could hear the scratching of their claws upon the fenders and the roof.

He switched off the lights and killed the engine, tossed the empty can into the waste box. He pushed the "Recline" button on the side of the seat, leaned back, and closed his eyes.

He was awakened by the blowing of horns. It was still night, and the panel clock showed him that he had slept for a little over three hours.

He stretched, sat up, adjusted the seat. The other cars had moved up, and one stood to either side of him. He leaned on his own horn twice and started his engine. He switched on the forward lights and considered the prospect before him as he drew on his gloves.

Smoke still rose from the blackened field, and far off to his right there was a glow, as if the fire still continued somewhere in the distance. They were in the place that had once been known as Nevada.

He rubbed his eyes and scratched his nose, then blew the horn once and engaged the gears.

He moved forward slowly. The burned-out area seemed fairly level, and his tires were thick.

He entered the black field, and his screens were immediately obscured by the rush of ashes and smoke which rose on all sides.

He continued, hearing the tires crunching through the brittle remains. He set his screens at maximum and switched his headlamps up to full brightness.

The vehicles that flanked him dropped back perhaps eighty feet, and he dimmed the screens that reflected the glare of their lights.

He released a flare, and as it hung there, burning, cold, white, and high, he saw a charred plain that swept on to the edges of his eyes' horizon.

He pushed down on the accelerator, and the cars behind him swung far out to the sides to avoid the clouds that he raised. His radio crackled, and he heard a faint voice but could not make out its words.

He blew his horn and rolled ahead even faster. The other vehicles kept pace.

He drove for an hour and a half before he saw the end of the ash and the beginning of clean sand up ahead.

Within five minutes he was moving across desert once more, and he checked his compass and bore slightly to the west. Cars one and three followed, speeding up to match his new pace, and he drove with one hand and ate a corned-beef sandwich.

When morning came, many hours later, he took a pill to keep himself alert and listened to the screaming of the wind. The sun rose up like molten silver to his right, and a third of the sky grew amber and was laced with fine lines like cobwebs. The desert was topaz beneath it, and the brown curtain of dust that hung continuously at his back, pierced only by the eight shafts of the other cars' lights, took on a pinkish tone as the sun grew a bright red corona and the shadows fled into the west. He dimmed his lights as he passed an orange cactus shaped like a toadstool and perhaps fifty feet in diameter.

Giant bats fled south, and far ahead he saw a wide waterfall descending from the heavens. It was gone by the time he reached the damp sand of that place, but a dead shark lay to his left, and there was seaweed, seaweed, seaweed, fishes, driftwood all about.

The sky pinked over from east to west and remained that color. He gulped a bottle of ice water and felt it go into his stomach. He passed more cacti, and a pair of coyotes sat at the base of one and watched him drive by. They seemed to be laughing. Their tongues were very red.

As the sun brightened, he dimmed the screen. He smoked, and he found a button that produced music. He swore at the soft, stringy sounds that filled the cabin, but he didn't turn them off.

He checked the radiation level outside, and it was only a little above normal. The last time he had passed this way it had been considerably higher.

He passed several wrecked vehicles such as his own. He ran across another plain of silicon, and in the middle was a huge crater, which he skirted. The pinkness in the sky faded and faded and faded, and a bluish tone came to replace it. The dark lines were still there, and occasionally one widened into a black river as it flowed away into the east. At noon one such river partly eclipsed the sun for a period of eleven minutes. With its departure, there came a brief dust storm, and Tanner turned on the radar and his lights. He knew there was a chasm somewhere ahead, and when he came to it he bore to the left and ran along its edge for close to two miles before it narrowed and vanished. The other vehicles followed, and Tanner took his bearings from the compass once more. The dust had subsided with the brief wind, and even with the screen dimmed Tanner had to don his dark goggles against the glare of reflected sunlight from the faceted field he now negotiated.

He passed towering formations which seemed to be quartz. He had never stopped to investigate them in the past, and he had no desire to do it now. The spectrum danced at their bases, and patches of such light occurred for some distance about them.

Speeding away from the crater, he came again upon sand, clean, brown, white, dun, and red. There were more cacti, and huge dunes lay all about him. The sky continued to change, until finally it was as blue as a baby's eyes. Tanner hummed along with the music for a time, and then he saw the Monster.

It was a Gila, bigger than his car, and it moved in fast. It sprang from out the sheltering shade of a valley filled with cacti, and it raced toward him, its beaded body bright with many colors beneath the sun, its dark, dark eyes unblinking as it bounded forward on its lizard-fast legs, sable fountains rising behind its upheld tail, which was wide as a sail and pointed like a tent.

He couldn't use the rockets, because it was coming in from the side.

He opened up with his fifty-calibers and spread his "wings" and stamped the accelerator to the floor. As it neared, he sent forth a cloud of fire in its direction. By then, the other cars were firing, too.

It swung its tail and opened and closed its jaws, and its blood came forth and fell upon the ground. Then a rocket struck it. It turned, it leaped.

There came a booming, crunching sound as it fell upon the vehicle identified as car number one and lay there.

Tanner hit the brakes, turned, and headed back.

Car number three came up beside it and parked. Tanner did the same.

He jumped down from the cab and crossed to the smashed car. He had the rifle in his hands, and he put six rounds into the creature's head before he approached the car.

The door had come open, and it hung from a single hinge, the bottom one.

Inside, Tanner could see the two men sprawled, and there was some blood on the dashboard and the seat.

The other two drivers came up beside him and

stared within. Then the shorter of the two crawled inside and listened for the heartbeat and the pulse and felt for breathing.

"Mike's dead," he called out, "but Greg's starting to come around."

A wet spot that began at the car's rear end spread and continued to spread, and the smell of gasoline filled the air.

Tanner took out a cigarette, thought better of it, and replaced it in the pack. He could hear the gurgle of the huge gas tanks as they emptied themselves upon the ground.

The man who stood at Tanner's side said, "I never saw anything like it.... I've seen pictures, but— I never saw anything like it...."

"I have," said Tanner, and then the other driver emerged from the wreck, partly supporting the man he'd referred to as Greg.

The man called out, "Greg's all right. He just hit his head on the dash."

The man who stood at Tanner's side said, "You can take him, Hell. He can back you up when he's feeling better," and Tanner shrugged and turned his back on the scene and lit a cigarette.

"I don't think you should do—" the man began, and "Screw," said Tanner, and blew smoke in his face. He turned to regard the two approaching men and saw that Greg was dark-eyed and deeply tanned. Part Indian, possibly. His skin seemed smooth, save for a couple pockmarks beneath his right eye, and his cheekbones were high and his hair very dark. He was as big as Tanner, which was six-two, though not quite so heavy. He was dressed in overalls, and his carriage, now that he had had a few deep breaths of air, became very erect, and he moved with a quick, graceful stride.

"We'll have to bury Mike," the short man said.

"I hate to lose the time," said his companion, "but—" And then Tanner flipped his cigarette and threw himself to the ground as it landed in the pool at the rear of the car.

There was an explosion, flames, then more explosions. Tanner heard the rockets as they tore off toward the east, inscribing dark furrows in the hot afternoon's air. The ammo for the fifty-calibers exploded, and the hand grenades went off, and Tanner burrowed deeper and deeper into the sand, covering his head and blocking his ears against the noise.

As soon as things grew quiet, he grabbed for the rifle. But they were already coming at him, and he saw the muzzle of a pistol. He raised his hands slowly and stood.

"Why the goddamn hell did you do a stupid thing like that?" said the other driver, the man who held the pistol.

Tanner smiled, and, "Now we don't have to bury him," he said. "Cremation's just as good, and it's already over."

"You could have killed us all if those guns or those rocket launchers had been aimed this way!"

"They weren't. I looked."

"The flying metal could've—Oh. . . . I see. Pick up your damn rifle, buddy, and keep it pointed at the ground. Eject the rounds it's still got in it and put 'em in your pocket."

Tanner did this thing while the others talked.

"You wanted to kill us all, didn't you? Then you could have cut out and gone your way, like you tried to do yesterday. Isn't that right?"

"You said it, mister, not me."

"It's true, though. You don't give a good goddamn if everybody in Boston croaks, do you?"

"My gun's unloaded now," said Tanner.

"Then get back in your bloody buggy and get going! I'll be behind you all the way!"

Tanner walked back toward his car. He heard the others arguing behind him, but he didn't think they'd shoot him. As he was about to climb up into the cab, he saw a shadow out of the corner of his eye and turned quickly.

The man named Greg was standing behind him, tall and quiet as a ghost.

"Want me to drive awhile?" he asked Tanner, without expression.

"No, you rest up. I'm still in good shape. Later on this afternoon, maybe, if you feel up to it."

The man nodded and rounded the cab. He entered from the other side and immediately reclined his chair.

Tanner slammed his door and started the engine. He heard the air-conditioner come to life.

"Want to reload this?" he asked. "And put it back on the rack?" and he handed the rifle and the ammo to the other, who had nodded. He drew on his gloves then and said, "There's plenty of soft drinks in the fridge. Nothing much else, though," and the other nodded again. Then he heard car three start and said, "Might as well roll," and he put it into gear and took his foot off the clutch.

Charles Britt listened to the bell. His office was diagonally across the street from the cathedral, and each peal of the massive bell made his walls shake, and he was contemplating a lawsuit, for he maintained that its constant tolling had loosened his fillings and was causing his remaining teeth to ache.

He brushed a wisp of white hair back from his forehead and squinted through the bottom of his bifocals.

He turned a page in the massive ledger and lowered his head to read further.

Losses, all. If only he'd cornered the drug market. Patent medicines and aspirin seemed the only things that were selling just then.

Clothing was out. Everyone was making do with what he had. Foodstuffs were all suspect. Hardwares were doing very poorly, for few repairs were being made these days. Why bother?

He was in deeply when it came to clothing, foodstuffs, and hardware.

He muttered a curse and turned the page.

Nobody was working, nobody was buying. Three ships waited in the harbor, unable to unload their cargoes, *his* cargoes, because of the quarantine.

And the looting! He'd saved three extra damns

for the looters. He was sure that the insurance companies would find a way to renege. He was sure because there was a lot of Britt money in insurance. At least the police were shooting to kill when it came to the looters. He smiled at that.

A light rain stippled his window, melted the cathedral beyond it. He felt a small pity for the wet town crier, whose bawled "Oyez! Oyez! Oyez!" rang now across the square, competing with the monotonous tolling of the death bell. This, because he, Charles Britt, had once been town crier, many years ago when his pants had been short and his eyes unimprisoned by spectacles and ledgers, and in those days he had hated the rain.

Nobody was riding in his taxis. The hearses and the ambulances had all the business this day, and he owned neither.

Nobody was buying guns and ammunition. With the reduced population, there were now enough to go around, for all who desired to offend or defend.

Nobody was visiting his movie houses, for there was drama enough, and pathos, to fill each human life this day.

And nobody, nobody, but nobody, was buying the last edition of his newspaper—a special, at that—for which he had driven his decimated staff to heroic ends, not to mention himself, what with the double-time he'd paid them to produce the thing. The Plague Edition, it had been, with an attractive black-bordered front page; an exclusive article on "The Plague Throughout History," by a professor at Harvard, yet; a medical article on the symptoms of bubonic, pneumonic, and systemic plague, so you'd know which variety you were coming down with; six and a half pages of obituaries; one hundred human-interest interviews with fathers, mothers, sisters, brothers, widows, and widowers; and a stirring editorial on the heroic drivers of the six doomed vehicles on their way to the west coast. He almost wept when he considered the stacks of these growing old in the warehouses, for nothing, but nothing, is so stale as a dated newsrag, even if it does have an attractive, black-bordered front page.

The only thing that made him smile again was the final page in the ledger. He'd managed at the last moment to corner sixty percent of the coffins in town, two florist shops—which were presently costing him dearly to keep open—and somewhat over five hundred cemetery plots. "Buy into a rising market," had always been his philosophy, not to mention his religion, sex, politics, and aesthetics. This, at least, would serve as a weight on the other side of the balance, possibly even net him a profit. If death is the wave of the future, ride it, he figured.

He tugged at his ear and listened again to the crier's words, half-hid among those of the bell.

"... there to be burned!"

This troubled him.

And as he heard the announcement repeated, he remembered the exclusive article on "The

Plague Throughout History," by the Harvard professor.

Funeral homes, hospitals, and morgues were now as packed as the old charnel houses had been. So in those days they had taken to . . . Yes.

". . . Mass cremations to avoid spread of the disease!" cried the boy. "The following three places have been chosen, and the dead will be delivered to these sites, there to be burned! Number one, Boston Common . . ."

Charles Britt closed his ledger, removed his glasses, and began to polish them.

He resolved to bring suit in the morning, as his jaws tightened upon the cold iron blade, relentless, and a metallic taste filled his mouth.

After they had driven for about half an hour, the man called Greg said to him, "Is it true what Marlowe said?"

"What's a Marlowe?"

"He's driving the other car. —Were you trying to kill us? Do you really want to skip out?"

Hell laughed, then, "That's right," he said. "You named it."

"Why?"

Hell let it hang there for a minute then said, "Why shouldn't I? I'm not anxious to die. I'd like to wait a long time before I try that bit."

Greg said, "If we don't make it, the population of the continent may be cut in half."

"If it's a question of them or me, I'd rather it was them."

"I sometimes wonder how people like you happen."

"The same way as anybody else, mister, and it's fun for a couple people for a while, and then the trouble starts."

"What did they ever do to you, Hell?"

"Nothing. What did they ever do *for* me? Nothing. Nothing. What do I owe them? The same."

"Why'd you stomp your brother back at the hall?"

"Because I didn't want him doing a damn fool thing like this and getting himself killed. Cracked ribs he can get over. Death is a more permanent ailment."

"That's not what I asked you. I mean, what do you care whether he croaks?"

"He's a good kid, that's why. He's got a thing for this chick, though, and he can't see straight right now."

"So what's it to you?"

"Like I said, he's my brother, and he's a good kid. I like him."

"How come?"

"Oh, hell! We've been through a lot together, that's all! What are you trying to do? Psychoanalzye me?"

"I was just curious."

"So now you know. Talk about something else if you want to talk, okay?"

"Okay. You've been this way before, right?"

"That's right."

"You been any farther east?"

"I've been all the way to the Missus Hip."

"Do you know a way to get across it?"

"I think so. The bridge is still up at Saint Louis."

"Why didn't you go across it the last time you went there?"

"Are you kidding? The thing's packed with cars full of bones. It wasn't worth the trouble to try to clear it."

"Why'd you go that far in the first place?"

"Just to see what it was like. I heard all these stories, and I wanted to take a look."

"What was it like?"

"A lot of crap. Burned-down towns, big craters, crazy animals, some people—"

"People? People still live there?"

"If you want to call them that. They're all wild and screwed up. They wear rags or animal skins, or they go naked. They threw rocks at me till I shot a couple. Then they let me alone."

"How long ago was that?"

"Six—maybe seven years ago. I was just a kid then."

"How come you never told anybody about it?"

"I did. A coupla my friends. Nobody else ever asked me. We were going to go out there and grab off a couple of the girls and bring them back, but everybody chickened out."

"What would you have done with them?"

Tanner shrugged. "I dunno. Screw 'em and sell 'em, I guess."

"You guys used to do that, down on the Barbary Coast—sell people, I mean—didn't you?"

Tanner shrugged again. "Used to," he said, "before the Big Raid."

"How'd you manage to live through that? I thought they'd cleaned the whole place out?"

"I was doing time," he said. "A.D.W."

"What's that?"

"Assault with a deadly weapon."

"What'd you do after they let you go?"

"I let them rehabilitate me. They got me a job running the mail."

"Oh, yeah, I heard about that. Didn't realize it was you, though. You were supposed to be pretty good—doing all right, and ready for a promotion. Then you kicked your boss around and lost your job. How come?"

"He was always riding me about my record, and about my old gang down on the Coast. Finally, one day I told him to lay off, and he laughed at me, so I hit him with a chain. Knocked out the bastard's front teeth. I'd do it again."

"Too bad."

"I was the best driver he had. It was his loss. Nobody else will make the Albuquerque run, not even today. Not unless they really need the money."

"Did you like the work, though, while you were doing it?"

"Yeah, I like to drive."

"You should probably have asked for a transfer when the guy started bugging you."

"I know. If it was happening today, that's probably what I'd do. I was mad, though, and I used to get mad a lot faster than I do now. I think I'm smarter these days than I was before."

"If you make it on this run and you go home afterward, you'll probably be able to get your job back. Think you'd take it?"

"In the first place," said Tanner, "I don't think we'll make it. And in the second, if we do make it and there's still people around the town, I think I'd rather stay there than go back."

Greg nodded.

"Might be smart. You'd be a hero. Nobody'd know much about your record. Somebody'd turn you on to something good."

"The hell with heroes," said Tanner.

"Me, though, I'll go back if we make it."

"Sail round Cape Horn?"

"That's right."

"Might be fun. But why go back?"

"I've got an old mother and a mess of brothers and sisters I take care of, and I've got a girl back there."

Tanner brightened the screen as the sky began to darken.

"What's your mother like?"

"Nice old lady. Raised the eight of us. Got arthritis bad now, though."

"What was she like when you were a kid?"

"She used to work during the day, but she cooked our meals and sometimes brought us candy. She made a lot of our clothes. She used to tell us stories, like about how things were before the war. She played games with us, and sometimes she gave us toys."

"How about your old man?" Tanner asked him after a while.

"He drank pretty heavy, and he had a lot of jobs, but he never beat us too much. He was all right. He got run over by a car when I was around twelve."

"And you take care of everybody now?"

"Yeah. I'm the oldest."

"What do you do?"

"I've got your old job. I run the mail to Albuquerque."

"Are you kidding?"

"No."

"I'll be damned! Is Gorman still the supervisor?"

"He retired last year, on disability."

"I'll be damned! That's funny. Listen, down in Albuquerque do you ever go to a bar called Pedro's?"

"I've been there."

"Have they still got a little blonde girl plays the piano? Named Margaret?"

"No."

"Oh."

"They've got some guy now. Fat fellow. Wears a big ring on his left hand."

Tanner nodded and downshifted as he began the ascent of a steep hill.

"How's your head now?" he asked when they'd reached the top and started down the opposite slope.

"Feels pretty good. I took a couple of your aspirin with that soda I had."

"Feel up to driving for a while?"

"Sure, I could do that."

"Okay, then." Tanner leaned on the horn and braked the car. "Just follow the compass for a hundred miles or so and wake me up. All right?"

"Okay. Anything special I should watch out for?"

"The snakes. You'll probably see a few. Don't hit them, whatever you do."

"Right."

They changed seats, and Tanner reclined the one, lit a cigarette, smoked half of it, crushed it out, went to sleep.

The bell drowned his every seventh word, but since he had said his words more than seven times over, nothing was really lost upon the eight steadfast listeners who huddled on the benches before him: five women and three men in various stages of age and distress. Others came, stood in the distance near to the streetlight, listened for a time, hurried on—for a light rain was beginning to fall. and that which he was saying was not altogether new.

His clerical collar was frayed, and there was a bandage about his right hand which seemed dirtier each time that he gestured with it, which was often.

His beard seemed recent, his black suit ancient.

"The marks are upon my body, ____ they tell me my days are ____!" he said, his eyes as dark

45

and moist as the night and the rain, as glistening as the streetlight. "And I say that it is ____ judgment. We are all of us, ____ and every one of us, man, ____, and child, judged in these, the ____ days, and found to be guilty! ____ is what caused this thing to ____ upon us, you may be sure! ____ and nothing else! You see it ____ day of your lives! And now ____ is angry, my brethren, for the ____ of which we are all mutually ____! You know this! I know it! ____ tells us of these days! Can ____ look about us and fail to ____ that the very words of the ____ are become an actuality in our ____? Of course not! This is because ____ ran like a beast too long, ____ and corrupting, and men turned to ____! No wonder then that the Beast ____, with seven heads and ten horns ____ them, rises us from the ocean, ____ the seven seals have been broken ____ the four horsemen out of the ____, whose names we all know as ____, that dreaded ravener of the countryside! ____, who followeth in the wake of him! ____, who lays his hand upon us! ____, the final, terrible one, who killeth! ____, all of these be here tonight! ____ has judged us, and now only ____ can save us from the awful ____ that lies upon all mankind! Yes! ____ is the answer, my brethren! True ____ may save us still, from the ____ into which will be cast all ____ who bear the mark of the ____ upon their hands and their foreheads! ____ has said so in the holy ____! Can we think otherwise? Can we ____ this? You know it in your hearts, ____! Let us join together and ____!"

He bowed his head then, winced as he clasped

his hands, and continued to fight with the bell, for he knew that the odds were six to one in his favor.

"How long? How long? Oh my ____!" he cried. "Until mankind will see the ever-present ____?"

And the heavens were full of signs, cryptic and undecipherable, as the blue lightning stalked from pole to pole.

Wondering, he licked the rain from his lips and swallowed, to ease the dryness of his throat.

When Greg awakened him, it was night. Tanner coughed and drank a mouthful of ice water and crawled back to the latrine. When he emerged, he took the driver's seat and checked the mileage and looked at the compass. He corrected their course and, "We'll be in Salt Lake City before morning," he said, "if we're lucky. —Did you run into any trouble?"

"No, it was pretty easy. I saw some snakes, and I let them go by. That was about it."

Tanner grunted and engaged the gears.

"What was that guy's name that brought the news about the plague?" Tanner asked.

"Brady or Brody or something like that," said Greg.

"What was it that killed him? He might have brought the plague to L.A., you know."

Greg shook his head.

"No. His car had been damaged, and he was all broken up—and he'd been exposed to radiation a lot of the way. They burned his body and his car, and anybody who'd been anywhere near him got shots of Haffikine."

"What's that?"

"That's the stuff we're carrying—Haffikine antiserum. It's the only cure for the plague. Since we had a bout of it around twenty years ago, we've kept it on hand and maintained the facilities for making more in a hurry. Boston never did, and now they're hurting."

"Seems kind of silly for the only other nation on the continent—maybe in the world—not to take better care of itself, when they knew we'd had a dose of it."

Greg shrugged. "Probably, but there it is. Did they give you any shots before they released you?"

"Yeah."

"That's what it was, then."

"I wonder where their driver crossed the Missus Hip? He didn't say, did he?"

"He hardly said anything at all. They got most of the story from the letter he carried."

"Must have been one hell of a driver, to run the Alley."

"Nobody's ever done it before, have they?"

"Not that I know of."

"I'd like to have met the guy."

"Me too, I guess."

"It's a shame we can't radio across country, like in the old days."

"Why?"

"Then he wouldn't of had to do it, and we could find out along the way whether it's really worth making the run. They might all be dead by now, you know."

"You've got a point there, mister, and in a day or so we'll be to a place where going back will be harder than going ahead."

Tanner adjusted the screen, as dark shapes passed.

"Look at that, will you!"

"I don't see anything."

"Put on your infras."

Greg did this and stared upward at the screen.

Bats. Enormous bats cavorted overhead, swept by in dark clouds.

"There must be hundreds of them, maybe thousands...."

"Guess so. Seems there are more than there used to be when I came this way a few years back. They must be screwing their heads off in Carlsbad."

"We never see them in L.A. Maybe they're pretty much harmless."

"Last time I was up to Salt Lake, I heard talk that a lot of them were rabid. Someday someone's got to go—them or us."

"You're a cheerful guy to ride with, you know?"

Tanner chuckled and lit a cigarette, and, "Why don't you make us some coffee?" he said. "As for the bats, that's something our kids can worry about, if there are any."

Greg filled the coffepot and plugged it into the dashboard. After a time it began to grumble and hiss.

"What the hell's that?" said Tanner, and he hit the brakes. The other car halted, several yards behind his own, and he turned on his microphone and said, "Car three! What's that look like to you?" and waited.

He watched them: towering, tapered tops that spun between the ground and the sky, wobbling from side to side, sweeping back and forth, about a mile ahead. It seemed there were fourteen or fifteen of the things. Now they stood like pillars, now they danced. They bored into the ground and sucked up yellow dust. There was a haze all about them. The stars were dim or absent above or behind them.

Greg stared ahead and said, "I've heard of whirlwinds, tornadoes—big, spinning things. I've never seen one, but that's the way they were described to me."

And then the radio crackled, and the muffled voice of the man called Marlowe came through: "Giant dust devils," he said. "Big, rotary sand-storms. I think they're sucking stuff up into the dead belt, because I don't see anything coming down—"

"You ever see one before?"

"No, but my partner says he did. He says the best thing might be to shoot our anchoring columns and stay put."

Tanner did not answer immediately. He stared ahead, and the tornadoes seemed to grow larger.

"They're coming this way," he finally said. "I'm not about to park here and be a target. I want to be able to maneuver. I'm going ahead through them."

"I don't think you should."

"Nobody asked you, mister, but if you've got any brains, you'll do the same thing."

"I've got rockets aimed at your tail, Hell."

"You won't fire them—not for a thing like this, where I could be right and you could be wrong—and not with Greg in here, too."

There was silence within the static, then, "Okay, you win, Hell. Go ahead, and we'll watch. If you make it, we'll follow. If you don't, we'll stay put."

"I'll shoot a flare when I get to the other side," Tanner said. "When you see it, you do the same. Okay?"

"Okay."

Tanner broke the connection and looked ahead, studying the great black columns, swollen at their tops. There fell a few layers of light from the storm which they supported, and the air was foggy between the blackness of their revolving trunks. "Here goes," said Tanner, switching his lights as bright as they would beam. "Strap yourself in, boy," and Greg obeyed him as the vehicle crunched forward.

Tanner buckled his own safety belts as they slowly edged ahead.

The columns grew and swayed as he advanced, and he could now hear a rushing, singing sound, as of a chorus of the winds.

He skirted the first by three hundred yards and continued to the left to avoid the one which stood before him and grew and grew. As he got by it,

51

there was another, and he moved farther to the left. Then there was an open sea of perhaps a quarter of a mile leading ahead and toward his right. He sped across it and passed between two of the towers that stood like ebony pillars a hundred yards apart. As he passed them, the wheel was almost torn from his grip and he seemed to inhabit the center of an eternal thunderclap. He swerved to the right then and skirted another, speeding.

Then he saw seven more and cut between two and passed about another. As he did, the one behind him moved in terrible spurts of speed. One passed before him, exhaled heavily and turned to the left.

He was surrounded by the final four, and he braked, so that he was thrown forward and the straps cut into his shoulder, as two of the whirlwinds shook violently. One passed before him, and the front end of his car was raised from off the ground.

Then he floored the gas pedal and shot between the final two, and they were all behind him.

He continued on for about a quarter of a mile, turned the car about, mounted a small rise, and parked.

He released the flare.

It hovered, like a dying star, for about half a minute.

He lit a cigarette as he stared back, and he waited.

He finished the cigarette.

52

Then, "Nothing," he said. "Maybe they wouldn't spot it through the storm. Or maybe we couldn't see theirs."

"I hope so," said Greg.

"How long do you want to wait?"

"Let's have that coffee."

An hour passed, then two. The pillars began to collapse, until there were only three of the slimmer ones. They moved off toward the east and were gone from sight.

Tanner released another flare, and still there was no response.

"We'd better go back and look for them," said Greg.

"Okay."

And they did.

There was nothing there, though, nothing to indicate the fate of car three.

Dawn occurred in the east before they had finished with their searching, and Tanner turned the car around, checked the compass, and moved north.

"When do you think we'll hit Salt Lake?" Greg asked him, after a long silence.

"Maybe two hours."

"Were you scared, back when you ran those things?"

"No. Afterward, though, I didn't feel so good."

Greg nodded.

"You want me to drive again?"

"No. I won't be able to sleep if I stop now. We'll

take in more gas in Salt Lake, and we can get something to eat while a mechanic checks over the car. Then I'll put us on the right road, and you can take over while I sack out."

The sky was purple again, and the black bands had widened. Tanner cursed and drove faster. He fired his ventral flame at two bats who decided to survey the car. They fell back, and he accepted the mug of coffee Greg offered him.

The sky was as dark as evening when they pulled into Salt Lake City. John Brady—that was his name—had passed that way but days before, and the city was ready for the responding vehicle. Most of its ten thousand inhabitants appeared along the street, and before Hell and Greg had jumped down from the cab after pulling into the first garage they saw, the hood of car number two was opened and three mechanics were peering at the engine.

One of the mechanics approached them. He was short and stained dark with sun and grease, so that his eyes appeared even paler than they were. He regarded the black-framed nails of the hand he had begun to extend, then jerked it back and wiped it on his green coveralls, grinning as he did so and revealing a row of gold-capped teeth.

"Hi. I'm Monk," he said. "You're the ones bound for Boston, huh?"

"Yeah."

"I'll have my boys go over everything. Probably take a couple hours. What're your names?"

"I'm Greg."

"Hell," said Tanner.

"Hell?"

"Hell," he repeated. "Where can we get breakfast?"

"There's a diner across the street. But judging from that mob outside, you'll never make it. Why don't I send one of the boys after some chow? You can eat it in the office."

"Okay."

"I thought they'd send more than one car."

"They did. We lost two."

"Oh. Sorry to hear. You know, I talked with that guy Brady when he passed through. He said Boston'd sent six cars. He sure looked bad, and his car looked like it'd been through a war. The President wanted him to stay—said we could send someone the rest of the way. But Brady wouldn't hear any of that. He'd driven this far, and by God he'd finish it, he said."

"Jerk," said Tanner.

"He pulled a gun when we tried to take him to a doctor. Wouldn't leave his car. I think he was off his rocker. That's why we sent a car of our own after he left, to be sure you'd get the message."

"What car?" said Greg.

"It didn't...?"

Greg shook his head.

Monk snatched a pack of cigarettes from his breast pocket. He offered them around, and his hand shook as he held the flame.

"I thought maybe our driver gave you the message."

"Only Brady," said Greg. "Nobody else."

"How is Brady?"

"Dead."

"His shielding was in bad shape when we serviced the car," he said. "The Geig went mad when we tried it inside. We wanted to give him another car, but he pulled this gun. By God, he'd have *his* car, he said, hot as it was. So we fixed the shielding, but it isn't that easy to decontaminate in a hurry. When he rode out of here he was like sitting in an oven. That's one of the reasons we sent Darver.... Let's go on into the office." He gestured toward a heavy green door. "Hey, Red!" he called out. As they moved toward it, a younger man who fit the description left a work bench and approached, wiping his hands on a gasoline-soaked rag.

"Yeah, Monk?"

"Go wash up and run across the street. Get these guys some breakfast and bring it back here. We'll be in the office."

"Okay. Where do I get the money?"

"Take a five out of the cash register and leave a note."

"Right," and he moved off toward a yellow-streaked sink set against the far wall.

They entered the office. Monk closed the green door behind them and waved toward the chairs.

"Make yourselves comfortable." He drew a venetian blind closed as he spoke, cutting off a view of four faces staring in. Then he leaned against a green and battered filing cabinet and sighed.

"I want to wish you the best of luck," he said. "Boy! You should have seen that Brady when he pulled in here! Like death warmed over!"

"All right!" said Greg. "Stop reminding us, huh?"

"Sorry. I didn't mean— You know..."

"Yeah, sure. Let's talk about something else."

Tanner chuckled and blew a smoke ring. "Think it'll rain today?" he asked.

Greg opened his mouth, then closed it and swallowed whatever he might have said.

Monk raised a slat of the blind and squinted out beneath it.

"There's a couple cops keeping the people out," he said, "and I see another trying to clear the way for a car. I think maybe it's the President's, but I can't tell for sure."

"What's he want?" asked Tanner.

"To welcome you and wish you luck, probably."

Greg ran his hand through his hair. "How about that, the President," he said.

"Screw," said Tanner.

Greg cleaned his fingernails with the edge of a matchbook. "We're celebrities," he said.

"Who needs it?"

"It doesn't hurt any."

"Yeah, it's the President," said Monk, dropping the slat. "I'll got out and meet him. He'll be here in a minute."

"Rather have breakfast," said Tanner as Monk left the room.

"Why've you got to be that way?" asked Greg.

"What way?"

"Obnoxious. The guy's a big wheel here, and he's coming over to say something nice to us. Why do you want to blast him?"

"Who said I'm going to blast him?"

"I can just tell."

"Well, you're wrong, citizen. I'm going to be the sweetest, nicest, ass-kissingest hero the bastard ever went to talk to, hoping that it would help to get him reelected, of course. Okay?"

"I don't give a damn."

Tanner chuckled again.

The noise level rose as a door opened somewhere in the building. Tanner ground his cigarette out on the concrete floor and lit another.

"Who'd want to be a President?" he asked, as somewhere a door banged closed.

Greg crossed the room to a water cooler, filled a paper cone, and drank. After a time they heard footsteps, and the door opened once again.

The President, who was a thin, balding man, hook-nosed, pink-faced, and smiling round pearly dentures, raised his right hand and said, "I'm Travis. I'm very glad to meet you boys and welcome you to Salt Lake."

"This is the President," said Monk, smiling and wiping his hands on his coveralls.

Tanner stood and extended his hand.

"My name's Tanner, sir. I'm honored to make your acquaintance. This is my friend Greg. I'm happy to see Salt Lake again. It looks better each time I come this way."

"Hello, Greg. —Oh, you've been this way before?"

"A considerable number of times. It's one of the reasons they passed over a lot of the other volunteers for this job and selected me. I did quite a bit of driving—before I retired, that is."

"Really?"

"Yes. I have a small ranch now and only a few servants, and I spend most of my time listening to classical music and reading philosophy. Sometimes I write poetry. When I heard about this thing, though, I knew that I owed it to humanity and to the nation of California to volunteer. After all, they've been pretty good to me. So that's how I find myself visiting your town once more."

"I admire your spirit, Mr. Tanner. —What led you to volunteer, Greg?"

"I—well—volunteered because— I'm a driver. I run the mail to Albuquerque. I've got a lot of experience."

"I see. Well, both of you are to be commended. If all goes as we expect it to, will you be coming back this way again?"

"I plan to, sir," said Tanner.

"Very good. I'd be happy to receive you anytime you're in town. Perhaps we can have dinner, and I can hear a full report of the trip."

"Our pleasure, sir. If you're ever out L.A. way, I trust you'll drop in and spend some time at the rancho?"

"Delighted."

Tanner smiled and flicked an ash on the floor.

"I'm a bit concerned as to our route after we leave here," he said.

"U.S. Forty is good for a distance—how far, though, nobody can tell you. There's been no reason for our drivers to push in that direction."

"I understand. Well, that's something. I was planning on trying Forty, and this confirms it. Thank you."

"Glad to be of help. Have you eaten yet?"

"A fellow who works here went out to get us something. He should be back soon. We have to hurry, you know."

"Yes, that's true. Well, if there's anything you need, let me know."

"Thank you."

He shook their hands again.

"As I said, good luck. A lot of folks will be hoping and praying for you here."

"That is appreciated, Mr. President."

"I'll be seeing you."

"Good morning."

"Good-bye."

He turned then and left, Monk following him out. Tanner began to laugh.

"Why'd you hand him that line of shit, Hell?"

"Because I knew he'd believe it."

"Why?"

"He wants everything to be nice. So I told him nice things, and he believed them. Why not? Dumb bastard actually believed somebody'd volunteer for this!"

"Some guys did, Hell."

"Then why didn't they let them drive?"

"They weren't good enough."

"That's probably why they volunteered. Now they can brag about it. See how he sucked up to me after I talked about humanity? I hate guys like that. They're all phonies."

"At least he went away with a good impression."

Tanner laughed again.

Then the door opened and Monk came in, followed by Red, who carried a large brown bag.

"I got your breakfasts here," he said, and to Monk, "Here's the change."

As they opened the bag, "I'll go help on the car while you're eating," Monk said, pocketing the change. "By the way, there's a guy named Blinky outside who says he knows you, Hell."

"Never heard of him."

"Okay, I'll send him away."

The door closed softly behind him, and they ate.

After a time the door inched slowly open and a tall, gaunt man with thick glasses and a lantern jaw and a mop of snowy hair looked in and then entered.

"Hi, Hell," he said.

"What do you want?"

"What've you got?"

"Nothing for you. Go away."

"Is that any way to talk to the guy who made you your fortune?"

"What fortune?"

"I heard the President talking about the place you've got out there on the coast. Very cool. You made most of your money dealing with me, you know."

"Get lost."

"What have you got with you this time?"

"Stuff for Boston."

"A guy like you wouldn't make the trip unless there was a profit in it. What else have you got?"

"If you're not out of here by the time I finish this piece of toast, I'm going to teach you a new way to hurt."

"You're not going to do business with anybody else in this town, Hell. What are you carrying? Candy bars and pot, as usual? Horse, maybe?"

Tanner stuffed the toast into his mouth and rose to his feet, drawing the SS dagger he carried in his boot as he stood.

"I guess your hearing is as bad as your eyes, Blinky," he said, tossing the blade into the air and catching it so that the skull touched his forearm and an inch of steel was extended between his thumb and first finger. He stepped forward then, and Blinky placed his left hand on the doorknob.

"You don't scare me, Hell. You need me in this town."

He swung his arm and slashed the man's left cheek.

"Why did you do that?" Blinky asked, without inflection.

"For the fun of it," said Tanner, and he kicked him in the shins.

As the man bent forward, Tanner raised his arm to cut again, but Greg seized his wrist.

"For Chrissake! Stop it!" he said, as Tanner drove his left fist into Blinky's stomach. "Just kick him out! Why cut him up!"

Still struggling to free his arm, Tanner brought his knee up hard.

Blinky groaned and fell forward.

Greg dragged Tanner away then, before he could kick the man in the ribs.

"Stop it, damn you! There's no call for what you're doing!"

"All right! But get him out of my sight!"

"Okay, I will. If you'll put that knife away."

"He's all yours."

Greg released him and raised the man from the floor. Tanner wiped his dagger on his trousers and resheathed it. Then he returned to his breakfast.

Greg half-carried, half-led the man from the office.

After several minutes he returned.

"I lied about what happened," he said, "and they believed me, maybe because that guy's got a record. But why did you do it?"

"He bugged me."

"Why?"

"He's a lousy pusher, and he wouldn't take no for an answer."

"That any reason to do what you did to him?"

"Also, it was fun."

"You're a miserable bastard."

"Your toast is getting cold."

"What would you have done if I hadn't stopped you? Killed him?"

"No. Probably pulled a couple of his teeth with those pliers over on the desk."

Greg seated himself and stared at his eggs.

"You've got to be a bit nuts," he finally said.

"Aren't we all?"

"Maybe. But that was so uncalled for . . ."

"Maybe you really don't understand, Greg. I'm an Angel. I'm the last Angel left alive. And I've been an Angel since before we switched our denim back to leather, because of the damn storms. Do you know what that means? I'm the last, and I've got a reputation to uphold. Nobody screws with us, or we walk on 'em, that's what it is. Now, this dumb pusher thought he could shove me around, because he's got some muscle outside somewhere, and he thought I'd be going out to make a delivery to somebody else. So he comes in and treats me like some square citizen. I gotta walk on him, don't you understand? I gave him a chance to shut up, and he didn't. Then it was a matter of honor. I had to stomp him."

"But you're not a club anymore. You're just one man."

"Ain't the last Catholic the Pope?"

"I guess so."

"Same thing, then."

"I don't think you're going to last very long, Hell."

"Neither do I. But I don't think you'll make it much longer."

He peeled the cover from the coffee container, took a drink, smacked his lips, and belched.

"Glad I finally nailed that bastard, too. Never liked him."

"Why did they have to pick you?"

"Cause I'm a good driver. I got us this far, you know."

Greg didn't answer, and Tanner rose and crossed to the window. He cracked the blinds and stared out.

"Crowd's thinning a bit," he said. "A lot of them have moved to the other side of the street and on up the block."

He stared at the clock and said, "I wish we were moving again. I hate to waste the daylight in this city."

Greg didn't reply, so Tanner opened a file drawer, stared within, closed it again. He took a drink of coffee. He lit a cigarette.

"I wonder how they're doing on the car?" he asked.

Greg finished eating and threw his empty containers into the wastebasket. He picked up Tanner's and threw them there too. "You're a slob," he said as he did so.

Tanner yawned and stared back out the window.

"I'm going to find the head," said Greg, and left him.

Then Tanner paced and smoked, and finally he went out to watch the men working on the car.

"How's it going?"

"Everything's okay so far. Did you see the guy who was hurt?"

"Yeah."

"He sure looked terrible, with all that blood."

"You going to change the oil?"

"Yeah."

"How much longer are you going to be?"

"Maybe an hour."

"Is there a back door to this place?"

"Go around that red car to the left. You'll see it then."

"Know if anybody's out there?"

"I don't think so. It's all weeds and our junk heap."

Tanner grunted and moved toward the back of the shop. He opened the door and looked outside, then stepped through it.

The air was warm, and though the odors of grease and banana oil and gasoline still clung lightly to it, he also smelled the smell that moist grass gives off on a warm evening, although it was not truly evening but black day at that time, as he stood there and looked about him until his eyes adjusted and he saw a narrow bench and moved to seat himself upon it, his back against the gray concrete, listening to the noises of the crickets in the weeds and lighting another cigarette and flipping the match toward the heap of fenders and axles and engine blocks all a-rust and amorphous beneath a single ribbon of twisted white that hung like a frozen thunderbolt in the blackness above his suddenly itching head; and scratching, he heard the cry of a bird above him in the painted fastness of an enormous tree whose branches dipped near the ground behind the rubbish; and slapping a mosquito, he felt a cool breeze suddenly touch his face, and with it came the promise of rain, which he did not altogether welcome; and as he double-inhaled the smoke of his cigarette and its tip grew bright, he threw a rock at a rat that darted from the junk heap, but missed it and snorted; and snorting, he wove within his mind the strands of violence past and fear like knowledge of trouble yet to come. Behind his eyes there was a vision of flames, flames encasing his car like the flower of death, two blackening skeletons within, as all the ammo in all the magazines expended itself in a series of mighty explosions, and all the squares who had ever hated him, signifying everybody, gibbered and jeered and shook billy clubs and moved in a wide, dancing circle about the pyre. "Damn you all," he said then softly, and the shock of white in the sky waved a little wider, bent like an upraised finger, and there came a peal of thunder like laughter. He allowed himself to think of the days when he had been Number One, and the thoughts troubled him. He'd missed the fire and the shooting on that night when they had raided the Coast and killed or carted off his entire pack. Ever since, he had been a country without a man. *That* had been his fire, and he'd missed the scene. Now another special fate, another special fire had fallen his lot—serving those who would have had him then. He missed his love, the one-eyed beacon of his life, his hog, with her four-speed Harley-Davidson transmission and stock clutch, two big H-D carburetors, and her throbbing, shuddering, exploding power between his thighs, bars in his hands and hellsmell of burned rubber and exhaust fumes peppering his nose around the smoke of his cigar. Gone. Forever. Impounded and sold to pay fines and costs. The way of all steel. The junk heap lay before him now. Who knew? The hog had been wife to him, damn near, and this might be her burial mound, with his own not too far east. He swore again and thought of his brother. It had been over a year since the last time he had seen him. There'd been a screen between them and a guard in the room, who had allowed cigarettes to change hands, and they hadn't had a whole big hell of a lot to talk about. Now his brother was probably taped up in bed someplace. Saved from the fire and the junk heap, which was something, anyway. He was the only square worth saving, Hell decided. Then he chain-lit another cigarette and flipped the butt toward the rubbish. A rat fled. He remembered his initiation. He'd been sixteen at the time. The bucket had been passed, and he'd stood tall and proud in his shiny jacket and gleaming irons, and though slightly drunk, he did not sway. One by one, they had urinated in the bucket. When they were finished, it was dumped over his head. That was his baptism, and he was an Angel. He wore the stinking garment for a year, and when two more had passed, he was nineteen and he was Number One. He had taken them on the rounds then, and everybody knew his name and stepped aside when they saw him coming. He was Hell, and his pack owned the Barbary Coast. They ranged where they would and did as they would, until he'd gotten into bad trouble and gone away and dark days came over the Coast. The town was perpetually initiated, as he had been, by rubbish from the heavens. *Their* pack was bigger, though, than his; and one day they had struck. His cell had been six by eight, and he'd shared it with a man who had liked little girls—well, if not too prudently. After trying to kill him, he'd found himself in solitary. At least he'd preferred it to the garbled ramblings of the wild-eyed, blue-eyed man they'd put him in with. Craig had sometimes foamed at the mouth, until Hell hit him in it one day and the foam turned red. They'd pried his fingers loose from his throat at the last minute, breaking one. They'd thought he'd go mad in solitary, himself, they later told him, after they'd released him into a full cell of his own, many months later. They'd thought he'd needed company, because he'd been a pack man. They didn't understand. They'd thought a gang of them was the Angels and a single Angel was a bum. They were wrong, though. He didn't go mad, or at least he wouldn't admit it if he had. He just sat there. He didn't play games, he didn't count numbers. He just sat there. He'd learned then that they couldn't hurt him. And he'd waited. For what, he hadn't known. This, though. This.

This was what he had waited for, as he'd sat there, dreaming of the Big Machine. What was it? Fire? Probably the fire, he decided, as he looked at the sky and sniffed. He slapped another mosquito. It still smelled like rain, and he wanted a drink. The cricket stopped, the birds stopped, as light poured into the world once more, white and bright and glaring. The skies opened as he sat there, like a sea of phosphorus washing out beyond its shores. Everything about him was suddenly limned in an unnatural brightness, and the bole of the great tree was shrunken by a brilliant entasis that attacked from the north. Every piece of scrap in the heap before him took on a life of its own, and he could almost, listening, hear the rubbish talk of its days and use and usefulness upon the remaining roads of the world. The rubbish spoke to him of the countryside, and he listened until the door beside him creaked and he heard Greg's voice.

"It's just about ready, Hell."

"Great."

"What're you doing out there?"

"Jackin' off in my mind."

The door slammed. Tanner sat there for a few more minutes, and a light rain began to fall, taking the bright gleam off the world, silencing the rubbish, drenching the bird in its tree and the rats in their lairs, tickling his face, spattering his boots, raising a smell like ashes from the earth. He stood then and entered the garage, shaking droplets from his beard.

"All set," said Monk, gesturing at the car. "Want to wait and see if the rain stops?"

"No. It'll probably start to get dark again soon."

"Probably."

They moved to a window. For the space of a few breaths, they watched the rain. Outside, the people still lined the streets.

"Dumb bastards," said Tanner. "Don't know enough to get in out of it."

"They're determined to see us off."

"Well, we'll give them a show then—lay down a little rubber. Might as well open the doors now, Monk."

"Thanks for the breakfast," said Greg.

"It's the least I could do."

"What happened to that guy?" Greg asked.

"Who?"

"Blinky. The one who had the accident."

"Oh. He's in the hospital. The cops took him in to get him patched up, and he had a heart attack there. They're giving him oxygen now. He was a small-town crook—record long as your arm. Not worth a damn. Can't say he's any loss."

"Too bad."

Monk shrugged. "That's what he gets for busting in and falling all over himself. So you're taking Forty, huh?"

Greg looked at Hell.

"That's right," Tanner said. "Who eats the Gila Monsters?"

"Huh?"

"We've got big snakes that the Gilas chomp up, along with a lot of other things, like bison and coyotes and God knows what all—and there's big bats that eat off the mutie fruit trees down Mexico way, and some freak spiders that feed on anything comes into their nets. But who eats the Gilas? A guy named Alex back home was telling me that since everything eats something else, then something had to have it in for the Gilas. I couldn't answer him, though. Do you know?"

"The butterflies," said Monk, "is what I've heard."

"Butterflies?"

"Yeah. You're lucky if you've never run into them. They're bigger than kites, and they settle down on the Gilas' necks and sting them half-dead. Then they lay their eggs. The caterpillars feed on the paralyzed lizards after they're hatched."

"I see."

"Then who eats the butterflies?" asked Greg.

"Damned if I know. Maybe the bats. That's a whole new world out there from what it was maybe a hundred years ago, and it's still changing fast. I doubt anybody knows what everything eats."

"Um-hm."

"I've got a hunch that anybody who goes looking will find that most of them will settle for humans in a pinch."

"Thanks," said Greg, "for everything. It's been nice knowing you, Monk."

"See you again." They shook hands.

"I doubt it," said Tanner. "I don't think I'll ever see you again. But thanks for the chow. Maybe you'll hear about us someday."

"Good luck. We're all pulling for you."

"You know what they call that," said Tanner, and he crossed the floor to their vehicle. He opened the door and climbed into the driver's seat. After a moment Greg entered from the other side.

"You didn't even shake his hand," he said.

"I don't hold with handshaking," said Tanner. "Most citizens couldn't care less when they do it. You stick out an empty hand, it once meant you didn't have a knife in it, that's all—and if you're left-handed, they're screwed. And vice-versa. Now, I'm left-handed, so I can do it and get away with it, but I still don't hold with it worth a damn. If there was ever anybody was my friend, he wouldn't have to shake hands with me to prove it. He'd know it, and I'd know it. And you know how it is, too. You meet somebody, and suddenly you both know you're somehow alike. No blood. Nothing. And you're buddies. No need for all that protocol crap that went out with the old age. That's all."

They locked the doors, and Tanner started the engine. He listened to its idling for a time, then switched on the view screens.

The big garage doors rattled open, and he beeped the horn once.

"Let's roll."

73

There was cheering as they rolled forth onto the street and sped away into the east.

"Could have used a beer," said Tanner. "Damn it!"

And they rushed along beside the remains of what had once been U.S. Route 40.

Tanner relinquished the driver's seat and stretched out on the passenger side of the cab. The sky continued to darken above them, taking upon it the appearance it had had in L.A. the day before.

"Maybe we can outrun it," Greg said.

"Hope so."

The blue pulse began in the north, flared into a brilliant aurora. The sky was almost black directly overhead.

"Run!" cried Tanner. "Run! Those are hills up ahead! Maybe we can find an overhang or a cave!"

But it broke upon them before they reached the hills. First came the hail, then the flak. The big stones followed, and the scanner on the right went dead. The sands blasted them, and they rode beneath a celestial waterfall that caused the engine to sputter and cough.

They reached the shelter of the hills, though, and found a place within a rocky valley where the walls jutted steeply forward and broke the main force of the wind/sand/dust/rock/water storm. They sat there as the winds screamed and boomed about them. They smoked and they listened.

"We won't make it," said Greg. "You were

right. I thought we had a chance. We don't. Everything's against us, even the weather."

"We've got a chance," said Tanner. "Maybe not a real good one. But we've been lucky so far. Remember that."

Greg spat into the waste container.

"Why the sudden optimism? From you?"

"I was mad before, and shooting off my mouth. Well, I'm still mad—but I got me a feeling now: I feel lucky. That's all."

Greg laughed. "The hell with luck. Look out there," he said.

"I see it," said Tanner. "This buggy is built to take it, and it's doing it. Also, we're only getting about ten percent of its full strength."

"Okay. but what difference does it make? It could last for a couple days."

"So we wait it out."

"Wait too long, and even that ten percent can smash us. Wait too long, and even if it doesn't, there'll be no reason left to go ahead. Try driving, though, and it'll flatten us."

"It'll take us ten or fifteen minutes to fix that scanner. We've got spare 'eyes.' If the storm lasts more than six hours, we'll start out anyway."

"Says who?"

"Me."

"Why? You're the one who was so hot on saving his own neck. How come all of a sudden you're willing to risk it, and mine too?"

Tanner smoked awhile, then said, "I've been thinking," and then he didn't say anything else.

75

"About what?" Greg asked him.

"Those folks in Boston," Tanner said. "Maybe it is worth it. I don't know. They never did anything for me. But hell, I like action, and I'd hate to see the whole world get dead. I think I'd like to see Boston, too, just to see what it's like. It might even be fun being a hero, just to see what that's like. Don't get me wrong. I don't give a damn about anybody up there. It's just that I don't like the idea of everything being like the Alley here—all burned out and screwed up and full of crap. When we lost the other car back in those tornadoes, it made me start thinking. . . . I'd hate to see everybody go that way—everything. I might still cop out if I get a real good chance, but I'm just telling you how I feel now. That's all."

Greg looked away and laughed, a little more heartily than usual.

"I never suspected you contained such philosophic depths."

"Me neither. I'm tired. Tell me about your brothers and sisters, huh?"

"Okay."

Four hours later, when the storm slackened and the rocks became dust and the rain fog, Tanner replaced the right scanner and they moved on out, passing later through Rocky Mountain National Park. The dust and the fog combined to limit visibility throughout the day. That evening they skirted the ruin that was Denver, and Tanner took over as they headed toward the place that had once been called Kansas.

He drove all night, and in the morning the sky was clearer than it had been in days. He let Greg snore on and sorted through his thoughts while he sipped his coffee.

It was a strange feeling that came over him as he sat there with his pardon in his pocket and his hands on the wheel. The dust fumed at his back. The sky was the color of rosebuds, and the dark trails had shrunk once again. He recalled the stories of the day when the missiles came down, burning everything but the northeast and the southwest; the day when the winds arose and the clouds vanished and the sky had lost its blue; the days when the Panama Canal had been shattered and radios had ceased to function; the days when the planes could no longer fly. He regretted this, for he had always wanted to fly, high, birdlike, swooping and soaring. He felt slightly cold, and the screens now seemed to possess a crystal clarity, like pools of tinted water. Somewhere ahead, far, far ahead, lay what might be the only other sizable pocket of humanity that remained on the shoulders of the world. He might be able to save it, if he could reach it in time. He looked about him at the rocks and the sand and the side of a broken garage that had somehow come to occupy the slope of a mountain. It remained within his mind long after he had passed it. Shattered, fallen down, half-covered with debris, it took on a stark and monstrous form, like a decaying skull which had once occupied the shoulders of a giant; and he pressed down hard on the accelerator, although it could go no farther. He began to tremble. The sky brightened, but he did not touch the screen controls. Why did he have to be the one? He saw a mass of smoke ahead and to the right. As he drew nearer, he saw that it rose from a mountain which had lost its top and now held a nest of fires in its place. He cut to the left, going miles, many miles, out of the way he had intended. Occasionally the ground shook beneath his wheels. Ashes fell about him, but now the smoldering cone was far to the rear of the right-hand screen. He wondered after the days that had gone before, and the few things that he actually knew about them. If he made it through, he decided he'd learn more about history. He threaded his way through painted canyons and forded a shallow river. Nobody had ever asked him to do anything important before, and he hoped that nobody ever would again. Now, though, he was taken by the feeling that he could do it. He wanted to do it. Damnation Alley lay all about him, burning, fuming, shaking, and if he could not run it, then half the world would die, and the chances would be doubled that one day all the world would be part of the Alley. His tattoo stood stark on his whitened knuckles, saying "Hell," and he knew that it was true. Greg still slept, the sleep of exhaustion, and Tanner narrowed his eyes and chewed his beard and never touched the brake, not even when he saw the rockslide beginning. He made it by and sighed. That pass was closed to him forever, but he had shot through without a scratch. His mind was an expanding bubble, its surfaces like the view screens, registering everything about him. He felt the flow of the air within the cab and the upward pressure of the pedal upon his foot. His throat seemed dry, but it didn't matter. His eyes felt gooey at their inside corners, but he didn't wipe them. He roared across the pocked plains of Kansas, and he knew now that he had been sucked into the role completely and that he wanted it that way. Damn-his-eyes Denton had been right. It had to be done. He halted when he came to the lip of a chasm, and headed north. Thirty miles later it ended, and he turned again to the south. Greg muttered in his sleep. It sounded like a curse. Tanner repeated it softly a couple times and turned toward the east as soon as a level stretch occurred. The sun stood in high heaven, and Tanner felt as though he were drifting bodiless beneath it, above the brown ground flaked with green spikes of growth. He clenched his teeth, and his mind went back to Denny, doubtless now in a hospital. Better than being where the others had gone. He hoped the money he'd told him about was still there. Then he felt the ache begin, in the places between his neck and his shoulders. It spread down into his arms, and he realized how tightly he was gripping the wheel. He blinked and took a deep breath and realized that his eyeballs hurt. He lit a cigarette and it tasted foul, but he kept puffing at it. He drank some water, and he dimmed the rearview screen as the sun fell behind him. Then he heard a sound like a distant rumble of thunder and was fully alert once more. He sat up straight and took his foot off the accelerator.

He slowed. He braked and stopped. Then he saw them. He sat there and watched them as they passed, about a half-mile ahead.

A monstrous herd of bison crossed before him. It took the better part of an hour before they had passed. Huge, heavy, dark, heads down, hooves scoring the soil, they ran without slowing, until the thunder was great, and then rolled off toward the north, diminishing, softening, dying, gone. The screen of their dust still hung before him, and he plunged into it, turning on his lights.

He considered taking a pill, decided against it. Greg might be waking soon, and he wanted to be able to get some sleep after they'd switched over.

He came up beside a highway, and its surface looked pretty good, so he crossed onto it and sped ahead. After a time, he passed a faded, sagging sign that said "Topeka—110 miles."

Greg yawned and stretched. He rubbed his eyes with his knuckles and then rubbed his forehead, the right side of which was swollen and dark.

"What time is it?" he asked.

Tanner gestured toward the clock in the dashboard.

"Morning or afternoon?"

"Afternoon."

"My God! I must have slept around fifteen hours!"

"That's about right."

"You been driving all that time?"

"That's right."

"You must be done in. You look like hell. Let me just hit the head. I'll take over in a few minutes."

"Good idea."

Greg crawled toward the rear of the vehicle.

After about five minutes, Tanner came upon the outskirts of a dead town. He drove up the main street, and there were rusted-out hulks of cars all along it. Most of the buildings had fallen in upon themselves, and some of the open cellars that he saw were filled with scummy water. Skeletons lay about the town square. There were no trees standing above the weeds that grew there. Three telephone poles still stood, one of them leaning and trailing wires like a handful of black spaghetti. Several benches were visible within the weeds beside the cracked sidewalks, and a skeleton lay stretched out upon the second one Tanner passed. He found his way barred by a fallen telephone pole, and he detoured around the block. The next street was somewhat better preserved, but all its storefront windows were broken, and a nude manikin posed fetchingly with her left arm missing from the elbow down. The traffic light at the corner stared blindly as Tanner passed through its intersection.

Tanner heard Greg coming forward as he turned at the next corner.

"I'll take over now," he said.

"I want to get out of this place first," and they

both watched in silence for the next fifteen minutes, until the dead town was gone from around them.

Tanner pulled to a halt then and said, "We're a couple hours from a place that used to be called Topeka. Wake me if you run into anything hairy."

"How did it go while I was asleep? Did you have any trouble?"

"No," said Tanner, and he closed his eyes and began to snore.

Greg drove away from the sunset, and he ate three ham sandwiches and drank a quart of milk before Topeka.

Tanner was awakened by the firing of the rockets. He rubbed the sleep from his eyes and stared dumbly ahead for about half a minute.

Like gigantic dried leaves, great clouds fell about them. Bats, bats, bats. The air was filled with bats. Tanner could hear a chittering, squeaking, scratching sound, and the car was buffeted by their heavy, dark bodies.

"Where are we?" he asked.

"Kansas City. The place seems full of them," and Greg released another rocket, which cut a fiery path through the swooping, spinning horde.

"Save the rockets. Use the fire," said Tanner, switching the nearest gun to manual and bringing cross-hairs into focus upon the screen. "Blast 'em in all directions—for five, six seconds—then I'll come in."

The flame shot forth, orange and cream

blossoms of combustion. When they folded, Tanner sighted in the screen and squeezed the trigger. He swung the gun, and they fell. Their charred bodies lay all about him, and he added new ones to the smoldering heaps.

"Roll it!" he cried, and the car moved forward, swaying, bat bodies crunching beneath its tires.

Tanner laced the heavens with gunfire, and when they swooped again, he strafed them and fired a flare.

In the sudden magnesium glow from overhead, it seemed that millions of vampire-faced forms were circling, spiraling down toward them.

He switched from gun to gun, and they fell about him like fruit. Then he called out, "Brake, and hit the topside flame!" and Greg did this thing.

"Now the sides! Front and rear next!"

Bodies were burning all about them, heaped as high as the hood, and Greg put the car into low gear when Tanner cried, "Forward!" and they pushed their way through the wall of charred flesh.

Tanner fired another flare.

The bats were still there, but circling higher now. Tanner primed the guns and waited, but they did not attack again in any great number. A few swept about them, and he took potshots at them as they passed.

Ten minutes later he said, "That's the Missouri River to our left. If we just follow alongside it now, we'll hit Saint Louis."

"I know. Do you think it'll be full of bats too?"

"Probably. But if we take our time and arrive with daylight, they shouldn't bother us. Then we can figure a way to get across the Missus Hip."

Then their eyes fell upon the rearview screen, where the dark skyline of Kansas City with bats was silhouetted by pale stars and touched by the light of the bloody moon.

After a time Tanner slept once more. He dreamed he was riding his bike, slowly, down the center of a wide street, and people lined the sidewalks and began to cheer as he passed. They threw confetti, but by the time it reached him it was garbage, wet and stinking. He stepped on the gas then, but his bike slowed even more and now they were screaming at him. They shouted obscenities. They cried out his name, over and over, and again. The Harley began to wobble, but his feet seemed to be glued in place. In a moment, he knew, he would fall. The bike came to a halt then, and he began to topple over toward the right side. They rushed toward him as he fell, and he knew it was just about all over....

He awoke with a jolt and saw the morning spread out before him: a bright coin in the middle of a dark-blue tablecloth, and a row of glasses along the edge.

"That's it," said Greg. "The Missus Hip."

Tanner was suddenly very hungry.

After they had refreshed themselves, they sought the bridge.

"I didn't see any of your naked people with spears," said Greg. "Of course, we might have passed their way after dark—if there are any of them still around."

"Good thing, too," said Tanner. "Saved us some ammo."

The bridge came into view, sagging and dark save for the places where the sun gilded its cables, and it stretched unbroken across the bright expanse of water. They moved slowly toward it, threading their way through streets gorged with rubble, detouring when it became completely blocked by the rows of broken machines, fallen walls, sewer-deep abysses in the burst pavement.

It took them two hours to travel half a mile, and it was noon before they reached the foot of the bridge, and, "It looks as if Brady might have crossed here," said Greg, eyeing what appeared to be a cleared passageway amidst the wrecks that filled the span. "How do you think he did it?"

"Maybe he had something with him to hoist them and swing them out over the edge. There are some wrecks below, down where the water is shallow."

"Were they there last time you passed by?"

"I don't know. I wasn't right down there by the bridge. I topped that hill back there," and he gestured at the rearview screen.

"Well, from here it looks like we might be able to make it. Let's roll."

They moved upward and forward onto the bridge and began their slow passage across the mighty Missus Hip. There were times when the bridge creaked beneath them, sighed, groaned, and they felt it move.

The sun began to climb, and still they moved forward, scraping their fenders against the edges of the wrecks, using their wings like plows. They were on the bridge for three hours before its end came into sight through a rift in the junkstacks.

When their wheels finally touched the opposite shore, Greg sat there breathing heavily and then lit a cigarette.

"You want to drive awhile, Hell?"

"Yeah. Let's switch over."

He did, and, "God! I'm bushed!" he said as he sprawled out.

Tanner drove forward through the ruins of East Saint Louis, hurrying to clear the town before nightfall. The radiation level began to mount as he advanced, and the streets were cluttered and broken. He checked the inside of the cab for radioactivity, but it was still clean.

It took him hours, and as the sun fell at his back, he saw the blue aurora begin once more in the north. But the sky stayed clear, filled with its stars, and there were no black lines that he could see. After a long while a rose-colored moon appeared and hung before him. He turned on the music, softly, and glanced at Greg. It didn't seem to bother him, so he let it continue.

The instrument panel caught his eye. The radiation level was still climbing. Then, in the forward screen, he saw the crater, and he stopped.

It must have been over half a mile across, and he couldn't tell its depth.

He fired a flare, and in its light he used the telescopic lenses to examine it to the right and to the left.

The way seemed smoother to the right, and he turned in that direction and began to negotiate it.

The place was hot! So very, very hot! He hurried. And he wondered as he sped, the gauge rising before him: What had it been like on that day, Whenever? That day when a tiny sun had lain upon this spot and fought with, and for a time beaten, the brightness of the other in the sky, before it sank slowly into its sudden burrow? He tried to imagine it, succeeded, then tried to put it out of his mind and couldn't. How do you put out the fires that burn forever? He wished that he knew. There'd been so many different places to go then, and he liked to move around.

What had it been like in the old days, when a man could just jump on his bike and cut out for a new town whenever he wanted? And nobody emptying buckets of crap on you from out of the sky? He felt cheated, which was not a new feeling for him, but it made him curse even longer than usual.

He lit a cigarette when he'd finally rounded the crater, and he smiled for the first time in months as the radiation gauge began to fall once more. Before many miles, he saw tall grasses swaying about him, and not too long after that he began to see trees. Trees short and twisted, at first, but the farther he fled from the place of carnage, the taller and straighter they became. They were trees such as he had never seen before—fifty, sixty feet in height—and graceful, and gathering stars, there on the plains of Illinois.

He was moving along a clean, hard, wide road, and just then he wanted to travel it forever—to Florida, of the swamps and Spanish moss and citrus groves and fine beaches and the Gulf; and up to the cold, rocky Cape, where everything is gray and brown and the waves break below the lighthouses and the salt burns in your nose and there are graveyards where bones have lain for centuries and you can still read the names they bore, chiseled there into the stones above them; down through the nation where they say the grass is blue; then follow the mighty Missus Hip to the place where she spreads and comes and there's the Gulf again, full of little islands where the old boosters stashed their loot; and through the shag-topped mountains he'd heard about: the Smokies, Ozarks, Poconos, Catskills; drive through the forest of Shenandoah; park, and take a boat out over Chesapeake Bay; see the big lakes and the place where the water falls, Niagara. To drive forever along the big road, to see everything, to eat the world. Yes. Maybe it wasn't all Damnation Alley. Some of the legendary places must still be clean, like the countryside about him now. He wanted it with a hunger, with a fire like that which always burned in his loins. He laughed then, just one short, sharp bark, because now it seemed like maybe he could have it.

The music played softly, too sweetly perhaps, and it filled him.

The bell that rang again, and yet again, did not completely submerge the sound of breaking glass. True, the silences came again, each deepened and intensified by memory and anticipation; but there had been that moment's pain within the already throbbing nervous system of the city.

The body moved to heal itself.

A light drizzle was descending, and the heavens flashed broken rainbows in all quarters. A downpour of dead fish, lasting perhaps a quarter of a minute, struck portions of the city, and telephone lines were draped with seaweed, and sand lashed against windowpanes. Sensing this provender, the rats came forth from the cellars and the barns, the sheds and the alleys, the junk heaps and the ditches, to feed upon the white-bellied manna, tails and whiskers twitching, eyes aglow, fur sleeked or rumpled by the wet; and when they departed, leaving the arrow-bodied skeletons white as ivory, some of them remained, like inkblots upon the lawns, the pavements, the porches, licking feebly at the raindrops.

But they had not broken the window, nor had the fish.

Sergeant Donahue, who was driving, turned to Lieutenant Spano at his right.

"No siren?" he queried.

"No siren."

Lieutenant Spano unfastened his black and gleaming holster, which he wore high upon his right hip.

"Turn out the lights."

The sergeant complied.

The world dimmed before them, and tiny dark shapes fled before the police cruiser. They turned the corner and slowed, both men studying the storefronts that lined this block of the city, the place where the wound had occurred.

"Ready with the spot."

"It's ready."

They cruised, silently, along the damp and glistening curb. A rumble of thunder came down from the north, with a flash of light that turned the sky into a yellow scroll covered with smoky hieroglyphs. For a moment the entire block was illuminated: cars, cables, hydrants, stores, trees, houses, and rats.

"There he is! Our side of the street! Hit him with the spot!"

Donahue turned on the spotlight and moved it. It fell upon the man before the broken window, bent forward, sack in hand, frozen in mid-reach.

"Don't move! You're under arrest!" he called over the loudspeaker.

The man turned and stared into the light. Then he dropped his sack and bounded into the street.

Lieutenant Spano fired six rounds from his .38 Special, and the man crumpled, fell, and lay like a dirty and wrung-out dishrag, his blood mingling with the moisture on the pavement, a dead rat at his right hand, a stripped fish above his head.

"You killed him," said Donahue, braking the car.

"He tried to escape," said Spano.

"We've got orders to try to bring them in."

"But he tried to escape."

"We're supposed to wound them, then, if we can."

"Yes, but he kept running after I hit him. He tried to escape."

Donahue met the other man's eyes, then looked away.

"He tried to escape," he agreed.

They left the car and approached the body. Spano turned it over.

"He's only a kid!" said Donahue. Then he moved to the sidewalk and opened the sack.

"Sporting goods," he said. "Softballs, a couple bats, a fielder's glove, and a catcher's mitt. Here's two footballs...A set of dumbbells— He was only a kid!"

Spano looked away. After a time he said, "He was looting."

"Yeah, and he tried to escape."

"Go see if you can get a call through to Precinct."

"Yeah. But I—"

"Donahue, shut up. You saw what happened."

"Yeah."

Spano lit a cigarette as the night became red

and unreal, and the crimson notes of the bell filled the world to its brim with their shudders.

Nine crawling rats, dragging their legs behind them, snapping at nothing, and wet, parlayed confusion and motion.

By morning he was into the place called Indiana and still following the road. He passed farmhouses which seemed in good repair. There could even be people living in them. He longed to investigate, but he didn't dare stop. Then after an hour, it was all countryside again, and degenerating.

The grasses grew shorter, shriveled, were gone. An occasional twisted tree clung to the bare earth. The radiation level began to rise once more. The signs told him he was nearing Indianapolis, which he guessed was a big city that had received a bomb and was now gone away.

Nor was he mistaken.

He had to detour far to the south to get around it, backtracking to a place called Martinsville in order to cross over the White River. Then as he headed east once more, his radio crackled and came to life. There was a faint voice, repeating, "Unidentified vehicle, halt!" and he switched all the scanners to telescopic range. Far ahead, on a hilltop, he saw a standing man with binoculars and a walkie-talkie. He did not acknowledge receipt of the transmission, but kept driving.

He was hitting forty miles an hour along a halfway decent section of roadway, and he gradually increased his speed to fifty-five, though the protesting of his tires upon the cracked pavement was sufficient to awaken Greg.

Tanner stared ahead, ready for an attack, and the radio kept repeating the order, louder now as he neared the hill, and called upon him to acknowledge the message.

He touched the brake as he rounded a long curve, and he did not reply to Greg's "What's the matter?"

When he saw it there, blocking the way, ready to fire, he acted instantly.

The tank filled the road, and its big gun was pointed directly at him.

As his eye sought for and found passage around it, his right hand slapped the switches that sent three armor-piercing rockets screaming ahead, and his left spun the wheel counterclockwise, and his foot fell heavy on the accelerator.

He was half off the road then, bouncing along the ditch at its side, when the tank discharged one fiery belch, which missed him and then caved in upon itself and blossomed.

There came the sound of rifle fire as he pulled back onto the road on the other side of the tank and sped ahead. Greg launched a grenade to the right and the left and then hit the fifty-calibers. They tore on ahead, and after about a quarter of a mile Tanner picked up his microphone and said, "Sorry about that. My brakes don't work," and hung it up again. There was no response.

As soon as they reached a level plain,

commanding a good view in all directions, Tanner halted the vehicle, and Greg moved into the driver's seat.

"Where do you think they got hold of that armor?"

"Who knows?"

"And why stop us?"

"They didn't know what we were carrying—and maybe they just wanted the car."

"Blasting it's a helluva way to get it."

"If they can't have it, why should they let us keep it?"

"You know just how they think, don't you?"

"Yes."

"Have a cigarette."

Tanner nodded, accepted.

"It's been pretty bad, you know?"

"I can't argue with that."

"...And we've still got a long way to go."

"Yeah, so we'd better get rolling."

"You said before that you didn't think we'd make it."

"I've revised my opinion. Now I think we will."

"After all we've been through?"

"After all we've been through."

"What more do we have to fight with?"

"I don't know yet."

"But, on the other hand, we know everything there is behind us. We know how to avoid a lot of it now."

Tanner nodded.

"You tried to cut out once. Now I don't blame you."

"You getting scared, Greg?"

"I'm no good to my family if I'm dead."

"Then why'd you agree to come along?"

"I didn't know it would be like this. You had better sense, because you had an idea what it would be like."

"I had an idea."

"Nobody can blame us if we fail. After all, we've tried."

"What about all those people in Boston you made me a speech about?"

"They're probably dead by now. The plague isn't a thing that takes its time, you know."

"What about that guy Brady? He died to get us the news."

"He tried, and God knows I respect the attempt. But we've already lost four guys. Now, should we make it six, just to show that everybody tried?"

"Greg, we're a lot closer to Boston than we are to L.A. now. The tanks should have enough fuel in them to get us where we're going, but not to take us back from here."

"We can refuel in Salt Lake."

"I'm not even sure we could make it back to Salt Lake."

"Well, it'll only take a minute to figure it out. For that matter, though, we could take the bikes for the last hundred or so. They use a lot less gas."

"And you're the guy was calling me names. You're the citizen was wondering how people like me happen. You asked me what they ever did to me. I told you, too: Nothing. Now maybe I want to do something for them, just because I feel like it. I've been doing a lot of thinking."

"You ain't supporting any family, Hell. I've got other people to worry about besides myself."

"You've got a nice way of putting things when you want to chicken out. You say, 'I'm not really scared, but I've got my mother and my brothers and sisters to worry about, and I got a chick I'm hot on. That's why I'm backing down. No other reason.'"

"And that's right, too! I don't understand you, Hell! I don't understand you at all! You're the one who put this idea in my head in the first place!"

"So give it back, and let's get moving."

He saw Greg's hand slither toward the gun on the door, so he flipped his cigarette into his face and managed to hit him once, in the stomach—a weak, left-handed blow, but it was the best he could manage from that position.

Then Greg threw himself upon him, and he felt himself borne back into his seat. They wrestled, and Greg's fingers clawed their way up his face toward his eyes.

Tanner got his arms free above the elbows, seized Greg's head, twisted, and shoved with all his strength.

Greg hit the dashboard, went stiff, then went slack.

Tanner banged his head against it twice more, just to be sure he wasn't faking. Then he pushed him away and moved back into the driver's seat. He checked all the screens while he caught his

breath. There was nothing menacing approaching.

He fetched cord from the utility chest and bound Greg's hands behind his back. He tied his ankles together and ran a line from them to his wrists. Then he positioned him in the seat, reclined it part way, and tied him in place within it.

He put the car into gear and headed toward Ohio.

Two hours later Greg began to moan, and Tanner turned the music up to drown him out. Landscape had appeared once more: grass and trees, fields of green, orchards of apples, apples still small and green, white farmhouses and brown barns far removed from the roadway he raced along; rows of corn, green and swaying, brown tassels already visible, and obviously tended by someone; fences of split timber, green hedges, lofty, star-leafed maples, fresh-looking road signs, a green-shingled steeple from which the sound of a bell came forth.

The lines in the sky widened, but the sky itself did not darken, as it usually did before a storm. So he drove on into the afternoon, until he reached the Dayton Abyss.

He looked down into the fog-shrouded canyon that had caused him to halt. He scanned to the left and the right, decided upon the left, and headed north.

Again the radiation level was high. And he hurried, slowing only to skirt the crevices, chasms, and canyons that emanated from that dark, deep center. Thick yellow vapors seeped forth from some of these and filled the air before him. At one point they were all about him, like a clinging, sulfurous cloud, and a breeze came and parted them. Involuntarily, then, he hit the brake, and the car jerked and halted, and Greg moaned once more. He stared at the thing for the few seconds that it was visible, then slowly moved forward once again.

The sight was not duplicated for the whole of his passage, but it did not easily go from out of his mind, and he could not explain it where he had seen it. Yellow, hanging and grinning, he had seen a crucified skeleton there beside the Abyss. *People*, he decided; *that explains everything.*

When he left the region of fogs, the sky was still dark. He did not realize for a time that he was in the open once more. It had taken him close to four hours to skirt Dayton, and now as he headed across a blasted heath, going east again, he saw for a moment a tiny piece of the sun, like a sickle, fighting its way ashore on the northern bank of a black river in the sky, and failing.

His lights were turned up to their fullest intensity, and as he realized what might follow, he looked in every direction for shelter.

There was an old barn on a hill, and he raced toward it. One side had caved in, and the doors had fallen down. He edged in, however, and the interior was moist and moldy-looking under his lights. He saw a skeleton, which he guessed to be that of a horse, within a fallen-down stall.

He parked and turned off his lights and waited.

Soon the wailing came once more and drowned out Greg's occasional moans and mutterings. There came another sound, not hard and heavy like gunfire, as that which he had heard in L.A., but gentle, steady, and almost purring.

He cracked the door, to hear it better.

Nothing assailed him, so he stepped down from the cab and walked back a ways. The radiation level was almost normal, so he didn't bother with his protective suit. He walked back toward the fallen doors and looked outside. He wore the pistol behind his belt.

Something gray descended in droplets, and the sun fought itself partly free once more.

It was rain, pure and simple. He had never seen rain, pure and simple, before. So he lit a cigarette and watched it fall.

It came down with only an occasional rumbling, and nothing else accompanied it. The sky was still a bluish color beyond the bands of black.

It fell all about him. It ran down the frame to his left. A random gust of wind blew some droplets into his face, and he realized that they were water, nothing more. Puddles formed on the ground outside. He tossed a chunk of wood into one and saw it splash and float. From somewhere high up inside the barn he heard the sound of birds. He smelled the sick-sweet smell of decaying straw. Off in the shadows to his right he saw a rusted threshing machine. Some feathers drifted down about him, and he caught one in his hand and studied it. Light, dark, fluffy, ribbed. He'd never really looked at a feather before. It worked almost like a zipper, the way the individual branches clung to one another. He let it go, and the wind caught it, and it vanished somewhere toward his back. He looked out once more, and back along his trail. He could probably drive through what was coming down now. But he realized just how tired he was. He found a barrel and sat down on it and lit another cigarette.

It had been a good run so far, and he found himself thinking about its last stages. He couldn't trust Greg for a while yet. Not until they were so far that there could be no turning back. Then they'd need each other so badly that he could turn him loose. He hoped he hadn't scrambled his brains completely. He didn't know what more the Alley held. If the storms were less from here on in, however, that would be a big help.

He heard a chuckle and was on his feet, the gun in his hand.

There was no one in sight. It didn't sound as if it had come from the car, and it didn't sound like Greg's voice anyway.

It had come from within the barn, though.

With his eyes, he explored each pool of shadow. Nothing.

Then it came again, and this time his eyes moved upward.

There was a loft.

He raised the pistol toward the opening to the rear of the building and up. He pointed it toward the dark oblong framed with straw.

"Come down!" he said.

There was no reply, not until he'd fired two shots through the opening, and then a, "Wait! I'm coming!" was their echo.

The man who hurried down the crosswise slats was covered with dark hair and rags. He was perhaps a foot shorter than Tanner, and he crouched with his back against the wall, shaking. His eyes were feral, and he held his hands before his chest, fingers hooking outward like claws.

"Who're you?"

The man's eyes darted from the barrel of the gun to Tanner's face and back again several times.

"I said, 'Who are you?', mister!"

"Kanis," said the man, "Geoffrey Kanis," and his voice was steady and loud. "I'm not a scientist," he added.

"Who the hell cares? What were you doing up there—besides watching me?"

"I came here when the rain started, to get out of it."

"What was so damned funny?"

"What do you mean?"

"Why were you laughing?"

"Oh. Because you don't follow the rules of Batesian mimicry—and you should, you know."

"What are you talking about?"

"I'm not a scientist."

"You said that already."

The man giggled, then recited, "It takes place in the same region and at the same season, according to Bates, and the mimicking species must not itself be protected, according to Bates, and it must be rarer than its model, Bates says, and it must differ from its own species by external characteristics clearly visible and able to create an illusion—Bates says that, too—and its mimicking characteristics should be only superficial and should produce no fundamental change in the species, Bates notes. He worked with butterflies, you know."

"Are you nuts?"

"Yes, but I follow the rules."

"Move over into the light, where I can see you better."

The man did.

"Yeah, you got a nutty look about you. What's this Bates crap?"

"It's a thing certain creatures do for purposes of self-protection: Batesian mimicry. They make themselves look like something they're not, so nothing will bother them. Now, if you had been smart, you'd never have grown that beard, you'd wash your face and comb your hair, you'd garb yourself in a dark suit and a white shirt and a necktie, and you'd carry a briefcase. You'd make yourself look like everybody else. Then nobody'd bother you. Then you could do whatever you wanted without molestation. You'd resemble the protected species. You wouldn't be forced into danger."

"How do you know I've been forced into danger?"

"There is a look about you, a smell, a certain jumpiness..."

"And if I'd looked square, this wouldn't have happened?"

"Probably not."

"What's your excuse?"

The man laughed, seemed to relax.

"Do you hate scientists?"

"No more than anybody else."

"What if I were a scientist?"

"Nothing."

"Okay. I'm a scientist."

"So what?"

"They lumped us all together. I'm a biologist."

"I don't dig you."

"It was the physicists who did this to us"—he gestured upward, outward—"and some chemists and mathematicians. Not the biologists."

"You mean the war?"

"Yes. No! I mean the world, the way it is now."

"I wasn't around when it happened. I don't know. Or care. What're you trying to say?"

"You shouldn't have blamed all the professors in all the disciplines for what happened."

"I didn't. I don't. I don't even know what happened. Not really. What *did* happen?"

"War, that's all. Mad and devastating. Lots of bombs and rockets, with a result nobody had predicted: This!" He gestured toward the outside once more. "Then what happened? Why, the survivors visited the remaining universities that I

knew of and killed the remaining professors—
English, sociology, physics, it didn't matter what
they taught—because the professors had obviously been responsible, because they had been
professors. That's why Batesian mimicry means
so much to me. They shot them, they tore them
apart, they crucified them. But not me. No. Not
me. I was them, the mob. So I lived. I'm Biology,
Room six-oh-four, Benton Building." He laughed
again.

"You mean you helped them when they killed
your friends?"

"They weren't my friends. They were in
different disciplines. I hardly knew them."

"But you helped?"

"Of course. That's why I'm still alive."

"So how's life?"

The man raised his hands to his face and began
to dig his nails into his cheeks.

"I can't forget it," he finally said.

"So that's what your damned mimicry gets
you—hung up by trying to be something else, too
much. No thanks. I know what I am."

"What?"

"I'm me. I'm an Angel. I don't have to pretend
to be anything else. If they don't like me, they can
cut me down, if they're able to. So far, they
haven't been able to. So screw 'em all! I don't dig
this mimic bit. No thanks. Not at all. They can go
to hell, every motherin' one of 'em!"

"A species can't make it that way."

"Screw species. I'm out to preserve me."

"That's the wrong attitude."

"Who says?"

"I don't know anymore." He continued to knead his cheeks, till the blood came forth and made his beard glisten.

"Stop that! You're bugging me! Where do you live, anyway?"

"Noplace, everyplace—I wander. Wherever I try to stay, they drive me out after a time. It's not holy to be mad anymore."

"There are settlements around here? People?"

"Some, some..."

"Well, go mimic the people living in one."

"I can't. I'm mad."

"Shave off your beard and bathe, and wear a dark suit and a white shirt and necktie, and carry a briefcase—"

"They don't look that way anymore—I forgot. All that is changed...."

"Well, go look however the hell they look."

"They all have beards, and they're dirty, and they wear old clothes."

"Then you're already mimicking them. So am I."

"No!"

"What's the difference, then?"

"We're mad!"

"Leave me out of this."

"But it's true. Who else but a madman would be in this old barn in the middle of a storm that could become holocaust? A sane man would have a home, a safe place—"

"Okay, you've got a point. I'm nuts too. Cigarette?"

"Yes, please."

Tanner tossed him the pack with his left hand, and then the matches. He held the gun steady with his right.

Kanis lit a cigarette and returned the pack and the matches the way they had come.

Tanner lit his own carefully, not taking his eyes off the smaller man.

"I'm curious about your form of madness, though," said the man. "I've never seen a vehicle like that before. That's radiation armor, isn't it?"

"Yes. I'm driving it to Boston."

"Silly thing to do. It's dangerous."

"I know. But the plague is there, and I'm carrying Haffikine antiserum."

"The plague? I knew it! I knew it would come!"

"Why?"

"Malthus and Darwin said so. We're all going to die! War and disease take care of the population-food ratio. But it's ceased to be a problem, and we're no longer fit to survive. So it will keep up until the job is finished."

"Nuts! They stopped the plague in L.A. That's why we had the serum out there."

"Then something else will come along."

Tanner shrugged. "I don't care what happens to them," he said.

"You're one of them, though."

"I am not. You said so yourself."

"I was wrong. I'm mad."

Tanner smoked awhile in silence.

"What are you going to do with me?" Kanis asked.

"Nothing. Keep pointing a gun at you till the storm lets up, because I don't trust you. Then I'm going to get into my car and drive away."

"Why don't you trust me? Because I'm a scientist?"

"Because you're mad."

"*Touché*. You could kill me, though."

"Why bother?"

"Maybe I want to be dead."

"Then do it yourself."

"I can't."

"Too bad."

"Would you take me with you to Boston?"

"Maybe. If you really wanted to go, and I thought I could trust you."

"Let me think about it."

"You asked me. Think all you want."

Tanner listened to the rain on the roof.

Finally, "No thanks," Kanis said. "They'd probably kill me, since I'm a scientist."

"I don't think so. They wouldn't in L.A. —But I thought you wanted to die?"

"Sometimes I do, and sometimes I don't. Have you got anything to eat? Anything you could spare? I'm terribly hungry?"

Tanner thought about it. He reviewed the contents of the refrigerator and the lockers.

"Okay," he said. "Walk ahead of me, and don't make any quick moves. I'll even leave you some rations."

Kanis preceded him, all the way to the car.

"Turn your back, and remember, there's a gun on it."

Kanis did an about-face.

Tanner crawled into the car, its door flung wide, and keeping his eye and his gun on the smaller man, he removed rations from their compartments and bore them back outside.

"Here. Have yourself a ball," he said, and he set the containers down on the floor of the barn and backed away.

He watched Kanis eat, until he couldn't believe that a man could be so hungry.

Then, "How do you feel?" he asked.

"A lot better, thanks."

"I'm sure they won't kill you in Boston," he said. "If you want to come along, I'll take you with me. What do you say?"

"No. Thanks. I feel better now."

"Why, for God's sake?"

"Because I've eaten."

"I mean, why won't you come along?"

"They'll hate me."

"No they won't."

"I helped, you know, when they burned the universities."

"So don't tell them about it."

He shook his head. "They'll know."

"How, you dumb bastard? Tell me *how*?"

"They'll know. *I* know."

"Man, you've got a guilt hang-up. I've heard of them, but I never believed it till now. Forget it! I'll take you there, you can do whatever you want to

108

your butterflies from now till hell freezes over, and nobody'll give a damn."

"No, thanks."

Tanner shrugged.

"Any way you want it."

There came a flash of blue lightning. The force of the downpour increased, until it sounded as if a thousand hammers fell upon the rooftop. An unnatural glow illuminated the barn for a time.

"What's *your* name?" Kanis asked.

"Hell."

"I knew it," he said. "Do you believe in God, Hell?"

"No."

"I didn't, but I do now. 'Forgive me my trespasses...'"

"Don't give me that lineup," said Tanner.

"I'm sorry. I—"

There came a rumble of thunder, which drowned out his following words.

Then, "...Kill me," said the man.

Tanner stepped on his cigarette butt.

"Will you?"

"What?"

"Kill me?"

"No."

"Why not?"

"Why should I?"

"I'd like it."

"Go to hell."

"I have."

"As you say, you're nuts."

"That is off the point."

"Do you want another cigarette?"

"No, thanks."

The rains relented a bit, and the thunders died. The lightnings fled away, and a natural quality of darkness returned to the quivering shadows.

"Okay, forget it," said Kanis.

"I already have."

"I don't mean to be a nuisance."

"I know. What do biologists do?"

"I've a doctor-of-philosophy degree in biological science. I'm a botanist, actually—"

"A doctor?"

"Yes."

"There's another guy inside my car, and he needs medical care. Will you take a look at him?"

"I'm not that kind of doctor."

"What do you mean?"

"I'm a doctor, but not a medical doctor. All I know about is botany."

"Biology is cutting up people and stuff like that, isn't it? Won't that help?"

"Not really. I don't know anything about medicine."

"Okay. I'll buy it. Too bad, though. He's bashed pretty bad."

"Sorry."

A certain brightness crept back into the day.

"Seems to be letting up," said Tanner.

"Yes."

"So I'll be going now."

"Now?"

"Why not?"

"It may start again."

"And then again, it may not. I'll have to take my chances."

Tanner backed toward the vehicle.

"Wait!"

"What?"

"Nothing."

Then Kanis lunged toward him, plunging his hand inside his shirt as he did so. Tanner fired twice.

"You damned fool! Why did you do that?" he cried, rushing to the fallen man's side.

Kanis coughed and spat blood.

"Why—not?" he asked. "We are all—mad...Hell!" and the rattle of his outgoing breath filled Tanner's ears.

"Crazy— Crazy..." said Tanner, and he dragged Kanis into the stall and laid him beside the skeleton of the horse. He searched him then and found that he bore no weapon.

"I wish you hadn't done that," he said, and then he returned to the barrel and sat down on it and lit another cigarette, his hand still feeling the impact of the hot and fired gun within it.

"Crazy," he repeated. "Absolutely out of his mind. Like, mad.

"That's what he was," he finally decided. "He was right."

He sat there for a long while, feeling the cold, moist breezes; and the rainfall lessened after a time, and he went back to the car and started it. Greg was still unconscious, he noted, as he backed out.

He took a pill to keep himself alert, and he ate some rations as he drove along. The rain continued to come down, but gently. It fell all the way across Ohio, and the sky remained overcast. He crossed into West Virginia at the place called Parkersburg, and then he veered slightly to the north, going by the old Rand McNally he'd been furnished. The gray day went away into black night, and he drove on.

There were no more of the dark bats around to trouble him, but he passed several more craters, and the radiation gauge rose, and at one point a pack of huge wild dogs pursued him, baying and howling, and they ran along the road and snapped at his tires and barked and yammered and then fell back. There were some tremors beneath his wheels as he passed another mountain, and it spewed forth bright clouds to his left and made a kind of thunder. Ashes fell, and he drove through them. A flash flood splashed over him, and the engine sputtered and died twice, but he started it again each time and pushed on ahead, the waters lapping about his sides. Then he reached higher, drier ground, and riflemen tried to bar his way. He strafed them and hurled a grenade and drove on by. When the darkness went away and the dim moon came up, dark birds circled him and dived down at him, but he ignored them, and after a time they, too, were gone.

He drove until he felt tired again, and then he

ate some more and took another pill. By then he was in Pennsylvania, and he felt that if Greg would only come around he would turn him loose and trust him with the driving.

He halted twice to visit the latrine, and he tugged at the golden band in his pierced left ear, and he blew his nose and scratched himself. Then he ate more rations and continued on.

He began to ache in all his muscles, and he wanted to stop and rest, but he was afraid of the things that might come upon him if he did.

As he drove through another dead town, the rains started again. Not hard, just a drizzly downpour, cold-looking and sterile—a brittle, shiny screen. He stopped in the middle of the road before the thing he'd almost driven into, and he stared at it.

He'd thought at first that it was more black lines in the sky. He'd halted because they'd seemed to appear too suddenly.

It was a spider's web, strands thick as his arm, strung between two leaning buildings.

He switched on his forward flame and began to burn it.

When the fires died, he saw the approaching shape, coming down from above.

It was a spider, larger than himself, rushing to check the disturbance.

He elevated the rocket launchers, took careful aim, and pierced it with one white-hot missile.

It still hung there in the trembling web and seemed to be kicking.

He turned on the flame again, for a full ten

seconds, and when it subsided, there was an open way before him.

He rushed through, wide-awake and alert once again, his pains forgotten. He drove as fast as he could, trying to forget the sight.

Another mountain smoked ahead and to his right, but it did not bloom, and few ashes descended as he passed it.

He made coffee and drank a cup. After a while it was morning and he raced toward it.

He was stuck in the mud, somewhere in eastern Pennsylvania, and cursing. Greg was looking very pale. The sun was nearing midheaven. He leaned back and closed his eyes. It was too much.

He slept.

He awoke and felt worse. There was a banging on the side of the car. His hands moved toward fire control and wing control automatically, and his eyes sought the screens.

He saw an old man, and there were two younger men with him. They were armed, but they stood right before the left wing, and he knew he could cut them in half in an instant.

He activated the outside speaker and the audio pickup.

"What do you want?" he asked, and his voice crackled forth.

"You okay?" the old man called.

"Not really. You caught me sleeping."

"You stuck?"

"That's about the size of it."

"I got a mule team can maybe get you out.

114

Can't get 'em here before tomorrow morning, though."

"Great!" said Tanner. "I'd appreciate it."

"Where you from?"

"L.A."

"What's that?"

"Los Angeles. West Coast."

There was some murmuring, then, "You're a long way from home, Mister."

"Don't I know it. —Look, if you're serious about those mules, I'd appreciate hell out of it. It's an emergency."

"What kind of?"

"You know about Boston?"

"I know it's there."

"Well, people are dying up that way, of the plague. I've got drugs here can save them, if I can get through."

There were some more murmurs, then, "We'll help you. Boston's pretty important, and we'll get you loose. Want to come back with us?"

"Where? And who are you?"

"The name's Samuel Potter, and these are my sons, Roderick and Caliban. My farm's about six miles off. You're welcome to spend the night."

"It's not that I don't trust you," said Tanner. "It's just that I don't trust anybody, if you know what I mean. I've been shot at too much recently to want to take the chance."

"Well, how about if we put up our guns? You're probably able to shoot us from there, ain't you?"

"That's right."

"So we're taking a chance just standing here.

We're willing to help you. We'd stand to lose if the Boston traders stopped coming to Albany. If there's someone else inside with you, he can cover you."

"Wait a minute," said Tanner, and he opened the door and jumped down.

The old man stuck out his hand, and Tanner took it and shook it, also his sons'.

"Is there any kind of doctor around here?" he asked.

"In the settlement—about thirty miles north."

"My partner's hurt. I think he needs a doctor." He gestured back toward the cab.

Sam moved forward and peered within.

"Why's he all trussed up like that?"

"He went off his rocker, and I had to clobber him. I tied him up, to be safe. But now he doesn't look so good."

"Then let's whip up a stretcher and get him onto it. You lock up tight then, and my boys'll bring him back to the house. We'll send someone for the doc. You don't look so good yourself. Bet you'd like a bath and a shave and a clean bed."

"I don't feel so good," Tanner said. "Let's make that stretcher quick, before we need two."

He sat up on the fender and smoked while the Potter boys cut trees and stripped them. Waves of fatigue washed over him, and he found it hard to keep his eyes open. His feet felt very far away, and his shoulders ached. The cigarette fell from his fingers, and he leaned backward on the hood.

Someone was slapping his leg.

He forced his eyes open and looked down.

"Okay," Potter said. "We cut your partner loose, and we got him on the stretcher. Want to lock up and get moving?"

Tanner nodded and jumped down. He sank almost up to his boot tops when he hit, but he closed the cab and staggered toward the old man in buckskin.

They began walking across country, and after a while it became mechanical.

Samuel Potter kept up a steady line of chatter as he led the way, rifle resting in the crook of his arm. Maybe it was to keep Tanner awake.

"It's not too far, son, and it'll be pretty easy going in just a few minutes now. What'd you say your name was, anyhow?"

"Hell," said Tanner.

"Beg pardon?"

"Hell. Hell's my name. Hell Tanner."

Sam Potter chuckled.

"That's a pretty mean name, mister. If it's okay with you, I'll introduce you to my wife and youngest as 'Mr. Tanner.' All right?"

"That's just fine," Tanner gasped, pulling his boots out of the mire with a sucking sound.

"We'd sure miss them Boston traders. I hope you make it in time."

"What do they do?"

"They keep shops in Albany, and twice a year they give a fair—spring and fall. They carry all sorts of things we need—needles, thread, pepper, kettles, pans, seed, guns and ammo, all kinds of things—and the fairs are pretty good times, too. Most anybody between here and there would help

117

you along. Hope you make it. We'll get you off to a good start again."

They reached higher, drier ground.

"You mean it's pretty clear sailing after this?"

"Well, no. But I'll help you on the map and tell you what to look out for."

"I got mine with me," said Tanner as they topped a hill, and he saw a farmhouse off in the distance. "That your place?"

"Correct. It ain't much farther now. Real easy walkin'—an' you just lean on my shoulder if you get tired."

"I can make it," said Tanner. "It's just that I had so many of those pills to keep me awake that I'm starting to feel all the sleep I've been missing. I'll be okay."

"You'll get to sleep real soon now. And when you're awake again, we'll go over that map of yours, and you can write in all the places I tell you about."

"Good scene," said Tanner, "good scene," and he put his hand on Sam's shoulder then and staggered along beside him, feeling almost drunk and wishing he were.

After a hazy eternity he saw the house before him, then the door. The door swung open, and he felt himself falling forward, and that was it.

Sleep. Blackness, distant voices, more blackness. Wherever he lay, it was soft, and he turned over onto his other side and went away again.

When everything finally flowed together into a

coherent ball and he opened his eyes, there was light streaming in through the window to his right, falling in rectangles upon the patchwork quilt that covered him. He groaned, stretched, rubbed his eyes, and scratched his beard.

He surveyed the room carefully: polished wooden floors with handwoven rugs of blue and red and gray scattered about them; a dresser holding a white enamel basin with a few black spots up near its lip where some of the enamel had chipped away; a mirror on the wall behind him and above all that; a spindly-looking rocker near the window, a print cushion on its seat; a small table against the other wall with a chair pushed in beneath it; books and paper and pen and ink on the table; a handstitched sampler on the wall asking God to bless; a blue-and-green print of a waterfall on the other wall.

He sat up, discovered he was naked, looked around for his clothing. It was nowhere in sight.

As he sat there, deciding whether or not to call out, the door opened and Sam walked in. He carried Tanner's clothing, clean and neatly folded, over one arm. In his other hand he carried his boots, and they shone like wet midnight.

"Heard you stirring around," he said, "How you feeling now?"

"A lot better, thanks."

"We've got a bath all drawn. Just have to dump in a couple of buckets of hot, and it's all yours. I'll have the boys carry it in in a minute, and some soap and towels."

Tanner bit his lip, but he didn't want to seem inhospitable to his benefactor, so he nodded and forced a smile then.

"That'll be fine."

".... And there's a razor and a scissors on the dresser—whichever you might want."

He nodded again. Sam set his clothes down on the rocker and his boots on the floor beside it, then left the room.

Soon Roderick and Caliban brought in the tub, spread some sacks and set it upon them.

"How you feeling?" one of them asked. (Tanner wasn't sure which was which. They both seemed graceful as scarecrows, and their mouths were packed full of white teeth.)

"Real good," he said.

"Bet you're hungry," said the other. "You slep' all afternoon yesterday, and all night, and most of this morning."

"You know it," said Tanner. "How's my partner?"

The nearer one shook his head, and, "Still sleeping and sickly," he said. "The Doc should be here soon. Our kid brother went after him last night."

They turned to leave, and the one who had been speaking added, "Soon as you get cleaned up, Ma'll fix you something to eat. Cal and me are going out now to try and get your rig loose. Dad'll tell you about the roads while you eat."

"Thanks."

"Good morning to you."

They closed the door behind them as they left.

Tanner got up and moved to the mirror, studied himself.

"Well, just this once," he muttered.

Then he washed his face and trimmed his beard and cut his hair.

Then, gritting his teeth, he lowered himself into the tub, soaped up, and scrubbed. The water grew gray and scummy beneath the suds. He splashed out and toweled himself down and dressed.

He was starched and crinkly and smelled faintly of disinfectant. He smiled at his dark-eyed reflection and lit a cigarette. He combed his hair and studied the stranger. "Damn! I'm beautiful!" he chuckled, and then he opened he door and entered the kitchen.

Sam was sitting at the table drinking a cup of coffee, and his wife, who was short and heavy and wore long gray skirts, was facing in the other direction, leaning over the stove. She turned, and he saw that her face was large, with bulging red cheeks that dimpled and a little white scar in the middle of her forehead. Her hair was brown, shot through with gray, and pulled back into a knot. She bobbed her head and smiled a "Good morning" at him.

"Morning," he replied. "I'm afraid I left kind of a mess in the other room."

"Don't worry about that," said Sam. "Seat yourself, and we'll have you some breakfast in a minute. The boys told you about your friend?"

Tanner nodded.

As she placed a cup of coffee in front of Tanner, Sam said, "Wife's name's Susan."

"How do," she said.

"Hi."

"Now, then, I got your map here. Saw it sticking out of your jacket. That's your gun hanging aside the door, too. Anyhows, I've been figuring, and I think the best way you could head would be up to Albany, and then go along the old Route Nine, which is in pretty good shape." He spread the map and pointed as he talked. "Now, it won't be all of a picnic," he said, "but it looks like the cleanest and fastest way in—"

"Breakfast," said his wife, and pushed the map aside to set a plateful of eggs and bacon and sausages in front of Tanner, and another one, holding four pieces of toast, next to it. There was marmalade, jam, jelly, and butter on the table, and Tanner helped himself to it and sipped the coffee and filled the empty places inside while Sam talked.

He told him about the gangs that ran between Boston and Albany on bikes, hijacking anything they could, and that was the reason most cargo went in convoys with shotgun riders aboard. "But you don't have to worry, with that rig of yours, do you?" he asked, and Tanner said, "Hope not," and wolfed down more food. He wondered, though, if they were anything like his old pack, and he hoped not, again, for both their sakes.

Tanner raised his coffee cup, and he heard a sound outside.

The door opened, and a boy ran into the kitchen. Tanner figured him as between ten and twelve years of age. An older man followed him, carrying the traditional black bag.

"We're here! We're here!" cried the boy, and Sam stood and shook hands with the man, so Tanner figured he should, too. He wiped his mouth and gripped the man's hand and said, "My partner sort of went out of his head. He jumped me, and we had a fight. I shoved him, and he banged his head on the dashboard."

The doctor, a dark-haired man, probably in his late forties, wore a dark suit. His face was heavily lined, and his eyes looked tired. He nodded.

Sam said, "I'll take you to him," and he led him out through the door at the other end of the kitchen.

Tanner reseated himself and picked up the last piece of toast. Susan refilled his coffee cup, and he nodded to her.

"My name's Jerry," said the boy, seating himself in his father's abandoned chair. "Is your name really Hell?"

"Hush, you!" said his mother.

"'Fraid so," said Tanner.

"...And you drove all the way across the country? Through the Alley?"

"So far."

"What was it like?"

"Mean."

"What all'd you see?"

"Bats as big as this kitchen—some of them even

bigger—on the other side of the Missus Hip. Lot of them in Saint Louis."

"What'd you do?"

"Shot 'em. Burned 'em. Drove through 'em."

"What else you see?"

"Gila Monsters. Big, Technicolor lizards—the size of a barn. Dust Devils—big circling winds that sucked up one car. Fire-topped mountains. Real big thorn bushes that we had to burn. Drove through some storms. Drove over places where the ground was like glass. Drove along where the ground was shaking. Drove around big craters, all radioactive."

"Wish I could do that someday."

"Maybe you will, someday."

Tanner finished the food and lit a cigarette and sipped the coffee.

"Real good breakfast," he called out. "Best I've eaten in days. Thanks."

Susan smiled, then said, "Jerry, don't pester the man."

"No bother, missus. He's okay."

"What's that ring on your hand?" said Jerry. "It looks like a snake."

"That's what it is," said Tanner, pulling it off. "It is sterling silver with red-glass eyes, and I got it in a place called Tijuana. Here. You keep it."

"I couldn't take that," said the boy, and he looked at his mother, his eyes asking if he could. She shook her head from left to right, and Tanner saw it and said, "Your folks were good enough to help me out and get a doc for my partner and feed me and give me a place to sleep. I'm sure they won't mind if I want to show my appreciation a little bit and give you this ring," and Jerry looked back at his mother, and Tanner nodded, and she nodded too.

Jerry whistled and jumped up and put it on his finger.

"It's too big," he said.

"Here, let me mash it a bit for you. These spiral kind'll fit anybody if you squeeze them a little."

He squeezed the ring and gave it back to the boy to try on. It was still too big, so he squeezed it again, and then it fit.

Jerry put it on and began to run from the room.

"Wait!" his mother said. "What do you say?"

He turned around and said, "Thank you, Hell."

"Mr. Tanner," she said.

"Mr. Tanner," the boy repeated, and the door banged behind him.

"That was good of you," she said.

Tanner shrugged. "He liked it," he said. "Glad I could turn him on with it."

He finished his coffee and his cigarette, and she gave him another cup, and he lit another cigarette. After a time Sam and the doctor came out of the other room, and Tanner began wondering where the family had slept the night before. Susan poured them both coffee, and they seated themselves at the table to drink it.

"Your friend's got a concussion," the doctor said. "I can't really tell how serious his condition is without getting X rays, and there's no way of getting them here. I wouldn't recommend moving him, though."

Tanner said, "For how long?"

"Maybe a few days, maybe a couple weeks. I've left some medication and told Sam what to do for him. Sam says there's a plague in Boston and you've got to hurry. My advice is that you go on without him. Leave him here with the Potters. He'll be taken care of. He can go up to Albany with them for the Spring Fair and make his way to Boston from there on some commercial carrier. He may be all right."

Tanner thought about it awhile, then nodded. "Okay," he said, "if that's the way it's got to be."

"That's what I recommend."

They drank their coffee.

Hell Tanner and Jerry Potter walked through the chill morning. Wisps of mist drifted along the ground, and the grass shone as if chrome-plated. There was a light haze in the air, and Jerry's breath crystallized as he blew it out before him, and he said, "Look, Hell! I'm smoking!"

"Yeah," said Tanner. "Wonder if my car's free yet."

"Probably," said Jerry. "That's a pretty good team." Then, "What do you do, Hell? I mean in real life, when you're not driving?"

"I'm always driving," said Tanner, "something or other. I'm a driver, that's all."

"You going to do more driving after you get to Boston?"

Tanner cleared his throat and spat against a tree.

"I don't know. Probably. Or else work someplace where they take care of cars and bikes."

"You know what I want to be?"

"No. Tell me."

"A pilot. I want to fly."

Tanner shook his head. "You can't. Do you ever watch the birds? They don't go very high. They're scared to. You get up there in a plane, and those winds'll kill you."

"I could fly real low..."

"The terrain is too irregular, and the winds vary in altitude. Hell, there are hills I won't drive on, because I might be swept away. You can tell them by the turbulence—the waves are visible, because of all the crud they carry—and also the fact that there's nothing but bare rock above a certain point."

"I could look out for stuff like that..."

"Yeah, but the winds change. They dip and they rise. There's no predicting when or where, either."

"But I *want* to fly."

Tanner looked at the boy and smiled. "There's an awful lot of things most people want to do, and it turns out for some reason or other they never can. Flying's one of them. You'll have to find something else."

Jerry's lower lip suddenly protruded, and he kicked at stones as he walked.

127

"Everybody has something special they want to do when they're young," said Tanner. "It never seems to work out that way, though. Either it turns out impossible, or you never get a chance to try it."

"What did you want to do, if it wasn't driving?"

Tanner stopped and turned his back to the wind, shielding the light he struck until he could get a cigarette going. Then he drew on it twice, staring into the smoke, and said, "I want to be the keeper of the machine."

"What machine?"

"*The* machine, the Big Machine. It's hard to explain . . ."

He closed his eyes a moment, then opened them, and, "I had a teacher," he said, "back when I was in school, who told us that the world was a big machine, that everything acted on everything else, that everything that happened was a function of all this action and interaction. So I started thinking about it, and I got me a picture of this goddamn big machine—all kinds of gears and pistons and chain belts; all sorts of levers and cams and shafts and pulleys and axles; and I figured it really existed someplace—this machine, I mean—and that according to whether it operated smoothly or not, things would go good or bad in the world. Well, I decided then that it wasn't running any too well and that it needed someone to give it a good going over and to keep an eye on it after that, once it was fixed. And I used to sit in class and have daydreams about it,

128

and think about it every night before I fell asleep. I used to think 'I'm going to go looking for it someday, and I'm going to find it. Then I'm going to be the keeper of the machine—the guy who oils it and tightens a nut here and there, replaces a worn part, polishes it, adjusts its controls. Then everything will work out all right. The weather will be nice, everybody will have enough to eat, there won't be any fighting, any sick people, any drunks, anybody who's got to steal because there's something he wants but can't have.' I used to think about that. I used to want that job. I could see me there, in a factory building or a big old cave, working my ass off to keep the thing in tiptop shape, and everybody happy. And I could see me having fun with it, too. Like, I'd want a vacation, say, so I'd turn it off and shut down the shop. Then everything'd stop, see? Except me. It'd be like you see in a photograph. Everybody'd be frozen, like statues, in whatever they were doing: driving along, eating, working, making love. Everything'd just stop, and I could walk through the city and nobody'd know I was there. I could see everybody at what they were up to. I could take food off their plates, swipe clothes and things from their stores, kiss their girls, read their books—for as long as I wanted. Then, when I got tired of that, I'd go back and turn the machine on, and everything'd start up again like natural, and no one'd be the wiser—and nobody'd care, even if they did know, because I'd keep the machine going real well and everybody'd be happy. That's what I wanted to be: the keeper of the Big Machine. Only I never found it."

"Did you ever go looking for it?" Jerry asked.

"No."

"Why not?"

"Because I wouldn't have found it."

"How do you know?"

"Because it isn't there. There is no machine. It was all a comparison. The teacher was just trying to say that life is *like* a big machine—not that that's what it is. I didn't understand him right, though, and I spent years thinking about the goddamn thing."

"How do you know there's no machine?"

"He explained what he'd meant to me later, when I went to ask him where the thing was. Boy, did I feel stupid!"

"He could have been wrong."

"Not a chance. They're too hip on stuff like that, those old teachers."

"Maybe he was lying."

"No. Now that I'm older, I know what he meant. He was wrong one way, though. It's too screwed up to be like a machine. But I know what he meant."

"Then they're not too hip, the teachers, if they can be wrong even one way."

They resumed walking again. Jerry looked at his ring. Tanner said, "They're hip in different ways. Like a biologist I met a while back. They're smart with words, mainly. My teacher knew what he was saying, and now I know. But it takes some getting older to figure what they're talking about."

"But what if he *was* wrong? What if it is there? And if you found it someday? Would you still do it? Would you still want to be the keeper of the machine?"

Tanner drew on his cigarette.

"There ain't no machine."

"But if there was?"

"Yeah, I guess so," he said. "I guess I'd still like the job."

"That's good, because I still want to fly, even though you told me I can't. Maybe the winds'll change someday."

Tanner put his hand on the boy's shoulder and squeezed it. "That'd be nice," he said.

"I hope you find it someday and fix everything—so I can fly, too."

Tanner flipped the butt into the ditch beside the road.

"If I ever do, that'll be the first thing I fix."

"Thank you, Hell."

Tanner jammed his hands into his pockets and hunched his shoulders against the wind. The sun rose a little higher, and the fog-snakes died beneath his heels.

Tanner regarded his freed vehicle, said, "I guess I'll be going, then," and nodded to the Potters. "Thanks," he said, and he unlocked the cab, climbed into it, and started the engine. He put it into gear, blew the horn twice and started to move.

In the screen, he saw the three men waving. He stamped the accelerator, and they were gone from sight.

He sped ahead, and the way was easy. The sky was salmon pink. The earth was brown, and there was much green grass. The bright sun caught the day in a silver net.

This part of the country seemed virtually untouched by the chaos that had produced the rest of the Alley. Tanner played music, drove along. He passed two trucks on the road and honked his horn each time. Once he received a reply.

He drove all that day, and it was well into the night when he pulled into Albany. The streets themselves were dark, and only a few lights shone from the buildings. He drew up in front of a flickering red sign that said, "Bar & Grill," parked, and entered.

It was small, and there was jukebox music playing, tunes he'd never heard before, and the lighting was poor, and there was sawdust on the floor.

He sat down at the bar and pushed the Magnum way down behind his belt so that it didn't show. Then he took off his jacket, because of the heat in the place, and he threw it on the stool next to him. When the man in the white apron approached, he said, "Give me a shot and a beer and a ham sandwich."

The man nodded his bald head and threw a shot glass in front of Tanner, which he then filled. Then he siphoned off a foam-capped mug and hollered over his right shoulder toward a window at his back.

Tanner tossed off the shot and sipped the beer. After a while, a white plate bearing a sandwich appeared on the sill across from him. After a longer while, the bartender passed, picked it up, and deposited it in front of him. He wrote something on a green chit and tucked it under the corner of the plate.

Tanner bit into the sandwich and washed it down with a mouthful of beer. He studied the people about him and decided they made the same noises as people in any other bar he'd ever been in. The old man to his left looked friendly, so he asked him, "Any news about Boston?"

The man's chin quivered between words, and it seemed a natural thing for him.

"No news at all. Looks like the merchants will close their shops at the end of the week."

"What's the last you heard of the situation there?"

"Folks keep dyin'. Other folks keep leavin' town, so's not to be caught by it. Dozens of 'em pass through here every day. There's a block up, up the road, for flaggin' 'em down to tell 'em they can't stop. So they go on through and stop

133

wherever they can find a settlement'll take 'em in. Also, there's a whole bunch of 'em that's taken to campin' up in the hills, thataway." He indicated the north. "It's three, four miles out of town. You can see their lights from the square."

"What's it like, the plague?"

"Ain't never seen a man die of it. But I hear tell he gets real thirsty and then starts to swell, under the arms and around the neck and down there—and then his lungs just fill with his own juices, and he drowns hisself."

"But there's still some people alive in Boston?"

"They keep comin'."

Tanner chewed his sandwich and thought of the plague. "What day is today?"

"Tuesday."

Tanner finished his sandwich and smoked a cigarette while he drank the rest of his beer.

Then he looked at the check, and it said, ".85."

He tossed a dollar bill on top of it and turned to go.

He had taken two steps when the bartender called out, "Wait a minute, mister."

He turned around.

"Yeah?"

"What you trying to pull?"

"What do you mean?"

"What do you call this crap?"

"What crap?"

The man waved Tanner's dollar at him, and he stepped forward and inspected it.

"Nothing wrong I can see. What's giving you a pain?"

"That ain't money. It's nothing."

"You trying to tell me my money's no good?"

"That's what I said. I never seen no bill like that."

"Well, look at it real careful. Read that print down there at the bottom of it."

The room grew quiet. One man got off his stool and walked forward. He held out his hand and said, "Let me see it, Bill."

The bartender passed it to him, and the man's eyes widened.

"This is drawn on the bank of the nation of California."

"Well, that's where I'm from," said Tanner.

"I'm sorry, it's no good here," said the bartender.

"It's the best I got," said Tanner.

"Well, nobody'll make good on it around here. You got any Boston money on you?"

"Never been to Boston."

"Then how the hell'd you get here?"

"Drove."

"Don't hand me a line of crap, son. Where'd you steal this?" It was the older man who had spoken.

"You going to take my money or ain't you?" said Tanner.

"I'm not going to take it," said the bartender.

"Then screw you," said Tanner, and he turned

and walked toward the door.

As always, under such circumstances, he was alert to sounds at his back.

When he heard the quick footfall, he turned. It was the man who had inspected the bill that stood before him, his right arm extended.

Tanner's right hand held his leather jacket, draped over his right shoulder. He swung it with all his strength, forward and down.

It struck the man on the top of his head, and he fell.

There came up a murmuring, and several people jumped to their feet and moved toward him.

Tanner dragged the gun from his belt and said, "Sorry, folks," and he pointed it, and they stopped.

"Now, you probably ain't about to believe me," he said, "when I tell you that Boston's been hit by the plague, but it's true, all right. Or maybe you will, I don't know. But I don't think you're going to believe that I drove here all the way from the nation of California with a car full of Haffikine antiserum. But that's just as right. You send that bill to the big bank in Boston, and they'll change it for you, all right, and you know it. Now, I've got to be going, and don't anybody try to stop me. If you think I've been handing you a line, you take a look at what I drive away in. That's all I've got to say."

And he backed out the door and covered it while he mounted the cab. Inside, he gunned the engine to life, turned, and roared away.

In the rearview screen he could see the knot of people on the walk before the bar, watching him depart.

He laughed, and the apple-blossom moon hung dead ahead.

Evelyn listened. Was she hearing things that weren't really there within the belltones? No. It came again, a knocking on the front door. She moved to the front of the room and looked out through the small window.

Then she unbolted the door and flung it wide.

"Fred!" she said. "This—"

"Back up!" he told her. "Quick! All the way across the room!"

"What's wrong?"

"Do it!"

She moved ten paces back, her eyes narrowing.

"Are your parents home?"

"No."

He stepped inside and closed the door behind him. He was eighteen years old, and his dark hair was straight and unruly. His angular jaw was clenched tight, his breathing was rapid, and his eyes drifted from place to place.

"What's the matter, Fred?"

"How do you feel?" he asked.

"I— Oh, no!"

He nodded. "I think I've got it. I had a fever earlier, and now I've got a chill. My armpits hurt, my throat is sore. No matter how much I drink, I still feel thirsty. That's why I don't want you to get near me."

Evelyn raised her hands to her cheeks and stared at him over the bright hedge of her nails. "After last night;" she said, "I . . . I haven't been feeling so good—either."

"Yeah," he said. "I probably killed you last night."

Evelyn was seventeen, had reddish hair, and her favorite color was green.

"How— What can we do?"

"Nothing," he said. "We can go to the clinic, and they can put us to bed and watch us die."

"Oh, no! Maybe the serum will come in time."

"Ha! I came to say good-bye, that's all. I love you. I'm sorry I gave it to you. Maybe if we hadn't done it— Oh, I don't know! I'm sorry, Evvie!"

She began to cry.

"Don't go!" she said.

"I've got to. Maybe you're only catching a cold or something. I hope so. Take some aspirin and go to bed."

He rested his hand on the doorknob.

"Don't go," she said.

"I've got to."

"To the clinic?"

"Are you kidding? They can't do anything. I'm just going—away . . ."

"What are you going to do?"

He looked away from her blue-green eyes.

"You know," he said. "I'm not going to go

through all that misery. I've seen people die of it. I'm not going to wait."

"Don't," she said. "Please don't."

"You don't know what it's like," he said.

"The serum may come. You ought to hold out for as long as you can."

"It won't come. You've heard what it's like out there. You know they won't make it."

"I think I've got it, too," she said. "So come here. It doesn't matter."

They met in the center of the room, and he wrapped his arms around her.

"Don't be afraid," she said. "Don't be afraid," and he held her for a long while, and then she took his hand and said, "Come this way. Don't be afraid. They won't be home for a long time," and she led him up to her bedroom and said, "Undress me," and he did.

They moved to the bed and did not speak again until after he had ridden her for several minutes and she heard him sigh and felt the warm moisture come into her. Then she rubbed his shoulders and said, "That was good."

"Yes." He raised himself to draw away then, and his elbow collapsed. "Oh, God!" he said. "I'm so weak all of a sudden!" He rolled to his side and swung his feet over the edge of the bed. He sat there and began to shake.

She draped a blanket over his shoulders and said, "You're thirsty, aren't you?"

"Yes."

"I'll get you a drink."

"Thanks."

He gulped the water she brought him. His head filled with bells as he drank it. "I love you," he said, and, "I'm sorry."

"Don't be. It was good."

Silently, he began to cry. She didn't realize it until his chest contracted about a sob, and she looked and saw that his face was wet.

"Don't cry," she said, "please..." and she wiped her eyes on a corner of the bedsheet.

"I can't help it. We're going to die."

"I'm afraid."

"So am I."

"What will it be like?"

"I don't know. Pretty bad, I guess. Don't think about it."

"I can't help it."

"I've got to lie down again. Excuse me. Do you have any other blankets?"

"I'll get some."

"... And another glass of water, please."

"Yes."

She returned and unfolded two wool blankets above him.

"That should be better."

She brought him another glass of water.

"Why should this happen to us?"

"I don't know. We're unlucky, that's all."

"You were going to—kill yourself. Weren't you?"

He nodded. "I still am—as soon as I feel a little

better. Ha! That sounds funny, doesn't it?"

"No. Maybe you're right—and it'll get worse from here on in."

"Stop it!"

"I can't help it. We're going to die; we know that. We might as well go as easy as possible. What were you going to do?"

"I was going to walk out on the bridge and stay there till I felt so bad that it would be worth it to go over the side."

"That's hard," she said, looking at her shadow on the wall.

"You got any better ideas?"

"No," she said, turning, so that light filtered through the venetian blinds fell upon her face and breast. Her zebra expression was indecipherable. "No."

"You sure?"

"No. I mean, maybe. My mother has some sleeping pills."

"Oh."

He stretched eight inches of blanket taut between his hands and bit down on the fabric.

"Get them," he said, "please."

"Are you sure?"

"No. But get them."

She left the room, returned after a few heartbeats with a small, dark bottle in one hand. "I have them here."

He took the bottle and stared at it. He turned it in his hand. He opened it. He removed a pill and held it in his palm, studying its contours.

"So that's it, huh?"

She nodded, biting her lip.

"How many would I have to take?"

"I read about someone taking twenty once. . . ."

"How many are there here?"

"I don't know."

Beads of perspiration appeared on his brow, and he cast the blankets aside. "Get me a glass of water," he said, bending forward and hugging his knees.

"All right."

She took the glass to the bathroom and refilled it. She placed it on the table beside the bed. She picked up the bottle, which had fallen among the blankets.

"Let's do it," he said.

"You sure?"

"I'm sure," he said. "It'll just be like going to sleep, won't it?"

"That's what they say."

"It seems like a better way out."

"Yes."

"Then count me out twenty pills."

She handed him the glass of water, and he held it in his right hand. Then he extended his left hand, palm upward.

She placed the pills within it.

He put two in his mouth and swallowed them with a gulp of water.

He made a face. "I always have a rough time swallowing pills," he said.

Then he took two more, and two more, and two more. "That's eight," he said.

He took them two at a time, five more times. "There were only eighteen," he said.

"I know."

"You said twenty."

"That's all there were, though."

"Christ! You mean I didn't leave any for you?"

"That's all right. I'll find another way. Don't worry."

"Oh, Evvie!" and he wrapped his arms about her waist, and she could feel his moist cheek against her belly. "I'm sorry, Evvie!" he said. "I didn't mean to! Honest!"

"I know. Don't worry. It'll be all right real soon. It should be real nice, just like going to sleep. I'm glad I had them for you. I love you, Fred!"

"I love you, Evvie! I'm sorry! Oh—"

"Why don't you just lie back and rest now?"

"I've got to go to the john first. All that water—" He climbed to his feet, one hand on the wall, and made his way out of the bedroom and into the hallway. He crossed into the bathroom and closed the door behind him.

She heard the water running, and she heard the toilet flush. She held her hands out before her and stared at her fingernails. Her lower lip was moist and tasted salty.

The water kept running, from bellnote through bellnote, and she thought of her parents, but she was still afraid to go and see.

Albany to Boston. A couple hundred miles. He'd managed the worst of it. The terrors of

Damnation Alley lay largely at his back now. Night. It flowed about him. The stars seemed brighter than usual. He'd make it, the night seemed to say.

He passed between hills. The road wasn't too bad. It wound between trees and high grasses. He passed a truck coming in his direction and dimmed his lights as it approached. It did the same.

It must have been around midnight that he came to the crossroads, and the lights suddenly nailed him from two directions.

He was bathed in perhaps thirty beams from the left and as many from the right.

He pushed the accelerator to the floor, and he heard engine after engine coming to life somewhere at his back. And he recognized the sounds.

They were all of them bikes.

They swung onto the road behind him.

He could have opened fire. He could have braked and laid down a cloud of flame. It was obvious that they didn't know what they were chasing. He could have launched grenades. He refrained, however.

It could have been him on the lead bike, he decided, all hot on hijack. He felt a certain sad kinship as his hand hovered above the fire control.

Try to outrun them, first.

His engine was open wide and roaring, but he couldn't take the bikes.

When they began to fire, he knew that he'd

have to retaliate. He couldn't risk their hitting a gas tank or blowing out his tires.

Their first few shots had been in the nature of a warning. He couldn't risk another barrage. If only they knew. . . .

The speaker!

He cut it in and mashed the button and spoke: "Listen, cats," he said. "All I got's medicine for the sick citizens in Boston. Let me through or you'll hear the noise."

A shot followed immediately, so he opened fire with the fifty-calibers to the rear.

He saw them fall, but they kept firing. So he launched grenades.

The firing lessened but didn't cease.

So he hit the brakes, then the flamethrowers. He kept it up for fifteen seconds.

There was silence.

When the air cleared, he studied the screens.

They lay all over the road, their bikes upset, their bodies fuming. Several were still seated, and they held rifles and pointed them, and he shot them down.

A few still moved, spasmodically, and he was about to drive on, when he saw one rise and take a few staggering steps and fall again.

His hand hesitated on the gearshift.

It was a girl.

He thought about it for perhaps five seconds, then jumped down from the cab and ran toward her.

As he did, one man raised himself on an elbow

and picked up a fallen rifle.

Tanner shot him twice and kept running, pistol in hand.

The girl was crawling toward a man whose face had been shot away. Other bodies twisted about Tanner now, there on the road, in the glare of the tail beacons. Blood and black leather, the sounds of moaning, and the stench of burned flesh were all about him.

When he got to the girl's side, she cursed him softly as he stopped.

None of the blood about her seemed to be her own.

He dragged her to her feet, and her eyes began to fill with tears.

Everyone else was dead or dying, so Tanner picked her up in his arms and carried her back to the car. He reclined the passenger seat and put her into it, moving the weapons into the rear seat, out of her reach.

Then he gunned the engine and moved forward. In the rearview screen he saw two figures rise to their feet, then fall again.

She was a tall girl, with long, uncombed hair the color of dirt. She had a strong chin and a wide mouth, and there were dark circles under her eyes. A single faint line crossed her forehead, and she had all of her teeth. The right side of her face was flushed, as if sunburned. Her left trouser leg was torn and dirty. He guessed that she'd caught the edge of his flame and fallen from her bike.

"You okay?" he asked when her sobbing had

diminished to a moist sniffing sound.

"What's it to you?" she said, raising a hand to her check.

Tanner shrugged. "Just being friendly."

"You killed most of my gang."

"What would they have done to me?"

"They would have stomped you, mister, if it weren't for this fancy car of yours."

"It ain't really mine," he said. "It belongs to the nation of California."

"This thing don't come from California."

"The hell it don't. I drove it."

She sat up straight then and began rubbing her leg.

Tanner lit a cigarette.

"Give me a cigarette?" she said.

He passed her the one he had lighted, lit himself another. As he handed it to her, her eyes rested on his tattoo.

"What's that?"

"My name."

"Hell?"

"Hell."

"Where'd you get a name like that?"

"From my old man."

They smoked awhile, then she said, "Why'd you run the Alley?"

"Because it was the only way I could get them to turn me loose."

"From where?"

"The place with horizontal venetian blinds. I was doing time."

"They let you go? Why?"

"Because of the big sick. I'm bringing in Haffikine antiserum."

"You're Hell Tanner."

"Huh?"

"Your last name's Tanner, ain't it?"

"That's right. Who told you?"

"I heard about you. Everybody thought you died in the Big Raid."

"They were wrong."

"What was it like?"

"I dunno. I was already wearing a zebra suit. That's why I'm still around."

"Why'd you pick me up?"

"Cause you're a chick, and cause I didn't want to see you croak."

"Thanks. You got anything to eat in here?"

"Yeah, there's food in there." He pointed to the refrigerator door. "Help yourself."

She did, and as she ate, Tanner asked her, "What do they call you?"

"Corny," she said. "It's short for Cornelia."

"Okay, Corny," he said. "When you're finished eating, you start telling me about the road between here and the place."

She nodded, chewed, and swallowed. Then, "There's lots of other gangs," she said. "So you'd better be ready to blast them."

"I am."

"Those screens show you all directions, huh?"

"That's right."

"Good. The roads are pretty much okay from

148

here on in. There's one big crater you'll come to soon, and a couple little volcanoes afterward."

"Check."

"Outside of them there's nothing to worry about but the Regents and the Devils and the Kings and the Lovers. That's about it."

Tanner nodded. "How big are those clubs?"

"I don't know for sure, but the Kings are the biggest. They've got a coupla hundred."

"What was your club?"

"The Studs."

"What are you going to do now?"

"Whatever you tell me."

"Okay, Corny. I'll let you off anywhere along the way that you want me to. If you don't want, you can come on into the city with me."

"You call it, Hell. Anywhere you want to go, I'll go along."

Her voice was deep, and her words came slowly, and her tone sandpapered his eardrums just a bit. She had long legs and heavy thighs beneath the tight denim. Tanner licked his lips and studied the screens. Did he want to keep her around for a while?

The road was suddenly wet. It was covered with hundreds of fishes, and more were falling from the sky. There followed several loud reports from overhead. The blue light began in the north.

Tanner raced on, and suddenly there was water all about him. It fell upon his car, it dimmed his screens. The sky had grown black again, and the banshee wail sounded above him.

He skidded around a sharp curve in the road. He turned up his lights.

The rain ceased, but the wailing continued. He ran for fifteen minutes before it built up into a roar.

The girl stared at the screens and occasionally glanced at Tanner. "What're you going to do?" she finally asked him.

"Outrun it, if I can," he said.

"It's dark for as far ahead as I can see. I don't think you can do it."

"Neither do I, but what does that leave?"

"Hole up someplace."

"If you know where, you show me."

"There's a place a few miles farther ahead—a bridge you can get under."

"Okay, that's for us. Sing out when you see it."

She pulled off her boots and rubbed her feet. He gave her another cigarette.

"Hey, Corny—I just thought—there's a medicine chest over there to your right. —Yeah, that's it. It should have some damn kind of salve in it you can smear on your face to take the bite out."

She found a tube of something and rubbed some of it into her cheek, smiled slightly, and replaced it.

"Feel any better?"

"Yes. Thanks."

The stones began to fall, the blue to spread. The sky pulsed, grew brighter.

"I don't like the looks of this one."

"I don't like the looks of any of them."

"It seems there's been an awful lot this past week."

"Yeah. I've heard it said that maybe the winds are dying down—that the sky might be purging itself."

"That'd be nice," said Tanner.

"Then we might be able to see it the way it used to look—blue all the time, and with clouds. You know about clouds?"

"I heard about them."

"White, puffy things that just sort of drift across—sometimes gray. They don't drop anything except rain, and not always that."

"Yeah, I know."

"You ever see any out in L.A.?"

"No."

The yellow streaks began, and the black lines writhed like snakes. The stonefall rattled heavily upon the roof and the hood. More water began to fall, and a fog rose up. Tanner was forced to slow, and then it seemed as if sledgehammers beat upon the car.

"We won't make it," she said.

"The hell you say. This thing's built to take it—and what's that off in the distance?"

"The bridge!" she said, moving forward. "That's it! Pull off the road to the left and go down. That's a dry riverbed beneath."

Then the lightning began to fall. It flamed, flashed about them. They passed a burning tree, and there were still fish in the roadway.

Tanner turned left as he approached the bridge.

He slowed to a crawl and made his way over the shoulder and down the slick, muddy grade.

When he hit the damp riverbed, he turned right. He nosed it in under the bridge, and they were all alone there. Some waters trickled past them, and the lightnings continued to flash. The sky was a shifting kaleidoscope, and constant came the thunder. He could hear a sound like hail on the bridge above them.

"We're safe," he said, and killed the engine.

"Are the doors locked?"

"They do it automatically."

Tanner turned off the outside lights.

"Wish I could buy you a drink, besides coffee."

"Coffee'd be good."

"Okay, it's on the way," and he cleaned out the pot and filled it and plugged it in.

They sat there and smoked as the storm raged, and he said, "You know, it's a kind of nice feeling being all snug as a rat in a hole while everything goes to hell outside. Listen to that bastard come down! And we couldn't care less."

"I suppose so," she said. "What're you going to do after you make it in to Boston?"

"Oh, I don't know.... Maybe get a job, scrape up some loot, and maybe open a bike shop or a garage. Either one'd be nice."

"Sounds good. You going to ride much yourself?"

"You bet. I don't suppose they have any good clubs *in* town?"

"No. They're all roadrunners."

"Thought so. Maybe I'll organize my own."

He reached out and touched her hand, then squeezed it.

"I can buy *you* a drink."

"What do you mean?"

She drew a plastic flask from the right side pocket of her jacket. She uncapped it and passed it to him.

"Here."

He took a mouthful and gulped it, coughed, took a second, then handed it back.

"Great! You're a woman of unsuspected potential and like that. Thanks."

"Don't mention it," and she took a drink herself and set the flask on the dash.

"Cigarette?"

"Just a minute."

He lit two, passed her one.

"There you are, Corny."

"Thanks. I'd like to help you finish this run."

"How come?"

"I got nothing else to do. My crowd's all gone away, and I've got nobody else to run with now. Also, if you make it, you'll be a big man. Like capital letters. Think you might keep me around after that?"

"Maybe. What are you like?"

"Oh, I'm real nice. I'll even rub your shoulders for you when they're sore."

"They're sore now."

"I thought so. Give me a lean."

He bent toward her, and she began to rub his

153

shoulders. Her hands were quick and strong.

"You do that good, girl.

"Thanks."

He straightened up, leaned back. Then he reached out, took the flask, and had another drink. She took a small sip when he passed it to her.

The furies rode about them, but the bridge above stood the siege. Tanner turned off the lights.

"Let's make it," he said, and he seized her and drew her to him.

She did not resist him, and he found her belt buckle and unfastened it. Then he started on the buttons. After a while he reclined her seat.

"Will you keep me?" she asked him.

"Sure."

"I'll help you. I'll do anything you say to get you through."

"Great."

"After all, if Boston goes, then we go too."

"You bet."

Then they didn't say much more.

There was violence in the skies, and after that came darkness and quiet.

When Tanner awoke, it was morning, and the storm had ceased. He repaired himself to the rear of the vehicle and after that assumed the driver's seat once more.

Cornelia did not awaken as he gunned the engine to life and started up the weed-infested slope of the hillside.

The sky was light once more, and the road was strewn with rubble. Tanner wove along it, heading toward the pale sun, and after a while Cornelia stretched.

"Ungh," she said, and Tanner agreed. "My shoulders are better now," he told her.

"Good," and Tanner headed up a hill, slowing as the day dimmed and one huge black line became the Devil's highway down the middle of the sky.

As he drove through a wooded valley, the rain began to fall. The girl had returned from the rear of the vehicle and was preparing breakfast when Tanner saw the tiny dot on the horizon, switched over to his telescopic lenses, and tried to outrun what he saw.

Cornelia looked up.

There were bikes, bikes, and more bikes on their trail.

"Those your people?" Tanner asked.

"No. You took mine yesterday."

"Too bad," said Tanner, and he pushed the accelerator to the floor and hoped for a storm.

They squealed around a curve and climbed another hill. His pursuers drew nearer. He switched back from telescopic to normal scanning, but even then he could see the size of the crowd that approached.

"It must be the Kings," she said. "They're the biggest club around."

"Too bad," said Tanner.

"For them or for us?"

"Both."

She smiled. "I'd like to see how you work this thing."

"It looks like you're going to get a chance. They're gaining on us like mad."

The rain lessened, but the fogs grew heavier. Tanner could see their lights, though, over a quarter-mile to his rear, and he did not turn his own on. He estimated a hundred to a hundred-fifty pursuers that cold, dark morning, and he asked, "How near are we to Boston?"

"Maybe ninety miles," she told him.

"Too bad they're chasing us instead of coming toward us from the front," he said, as he primed his flames and set an adjustment which brought cross-hairs into focus on his rearview screen.

"What's that?" she asked.

"That's a cross. I'm going to crucify them, lady," and she smiled at this and squeezed his arm.

"Can I help? I hate those bloody mothers."

"In a little while," said Tanner. "In a little while, I'm sure," and he reached into the rear seat and fetched out the six hand grenades and hung them on his wide, black belt. He passed the rifle to the girl. "Hang on to this," he said, and he stuck the .45 behind his belt. "Do you know how to use that thing?"

"Yes," she replied.

"Good."

He kept watching the lights that danced on the screen.

"Why the hell doesn't this storm break?" he said, as the lights came closer and he could make out shapes within the fog.

When they were within a hundred feet, he fired the first grenade. It arced through the gray air, and five seconds later there was a bright flash to his rear, burning within a thunderclap.

The lights immediately behind him remained, and he touched the fifty-calibers, moving the cross-hairs from side to side. The guns stuttered their loud syllables, and he launched another grenade. With the second flash, he began to climb another hill.

"Did you stop them?"

"For a time, maybe. I still see some lights, but they're farther back."

After five minutes, they had reached the top, a place where the fogs were cleared and the dark sky was visible above them. Then they started downward once more, and a wall of stone and shale and dirt rose to their right. Tanner considered it as they descended.

When the road leveled and he decided they had reached the bottom, he turned on his brightest lights and looked for a place where the road's shoulders were wide.

To his rear, there were suddenly rows of descending lights.

He found the place where the road was sufficiently wide, and he skidded through a U-turn until he was facing the shaggy cliff, now to his left, and his pursuers were coming dead on.

He elevated his rockets, fired one, elevated them five degrees more, fired two, elevated them another five degrees, fired three. Then he lowered them fifteen and fired another.

There were brightnesses within the fog, and he heard the stones rattling on the road and felt the vibration as the rockslide began. He swung toward his right as he backed the vehicle and fired two ahead. There was dust mixed with the fog now, and the vibration continued.

He turned and headed forward once more.

"I hope that'll hold 'em," he said, and he lit two cigarettes and passed one to the girl.

After five minutes they were on higher ground again, and the winds came and whipped at the fog, and far to the rear there were still some lights.

As they topped a high rise, his radiation gauge began to register an above-normal reading. He sought in all directions and saw the crater far off ahead. "That's it," he heard her say. "You've got to leave the road there. Bear to the right and go around that way when you get there."

"I'll do that thing."

He heard gunshots from behind him, for the first time that day, and though he adjusted the cross-hairs, he did not fire his own weapons. The distance was still too great.

"You must have cut them in half," she said, staring into the screen. "More than that. They're a tough bunch, though."

"I gather," and he plowed the field of mists and checked his supply of grenades for the launcher and saw that he was running low.

He swung off the road to his right when he began bumping along over fractured concrete. The radiation level was quite high by then. The crater was a thousand yards to his left.

The lights to his rear fanned out, grew brighter. He drew a bead on the brightest and fired. It went out.

"There's another down," he remarked as they raced across the hard-baked plain.

The rains came more heavily, and he sighted on another light and fired. It, too, went out. Now, though, he heard the sounds of their weapons about him once again.

He switched to his right-hand guns and saw the cross-hairs leap into life on that screen. As three vehicles moved in to flank him from that direction, he opened up and cut them down. There was more firing on his back, and he ignored it as he negotiated the way.

"I count twenty-seven lights," Cornelia said.

Tanner wove his way across a field of boulders. He lit another cigarette.

Five minutes later, they were running on both sides of him. He had held back again for that moment, to conserve ammunition and to be sure of his targets. He fired then, though, at every light within range, and he floored the accelerator and swerved around rocks.

"Five of them are down," she said, but he was listening to the gunfire.

He launched a grenade to the rear, and when he tried to launch a second, there came only a clicking sound from the control. He launched one to either side.

"If they get close enough, I'll show them some

fire," he said, and they continued on around the crater.

He fired only at individual targets then, when he was certain they were within range. He took two more before he struck the broken roadbed.

"Keep running parallel to it," she told him. "There's a trail here. You can't drive on that stuff till another mile or so."

Shots ricocheted from off his armored sides, and he continued to return the fire. He raced along an alleyway of twisted trees, like those he had seen near other craters, and the mists hung like pennons about their branches. He heard the rattle of the increasing rains.

When he hit the roadway once again, he regarded the lights to his rear and asked, "How many do you count now?"

"It looks like around twenty. How are we doing?"

"I'm just worried about the tires. They can take a lot, but they can be shot out. The only thing that bothers me is that a stray shot might clip one of the 'eyes.' Outside of that, we're bulletproof enough. Even if they manage to stop us, they'll have to pry us out."

The bikes drew near once again, and he saw the bright flashes and heard the reports of the riders' guns.

"Hold tight," he said, and he hit the brakes, and they skidded on the wet pavement.

The lights grew suddenly bright, and he unleashed his rear flame. As some bikes skirted him, he cut in the side flames and held them that way.

Then he took his foot off the brake and floored the accelerator without waiting to assess the damage he had done.

They sped ahead, and Tanner heard Cornelia's laughter.

"God! You're taking them, Hell! You're taking the whole damn club!"

"It ain't that much fun," he said. Then, "See any lights?"

She watched for a time, said, "No," then said, "Three," then, "Seven," and finally, "Thirteen."

Tanner said, "Damn."

The radiation level fell, and there came crashes amid the roaring overhead. A light fall of gravel descended for perhaps half a minute, along with the rain.

"We're running low," he said.

"On what?"

"Everything—luck, fuel, ammo. Maybe you'd have been better off if I'd left you where I found you."

"No," she said. "I'm with you, the whole line."

"Then you're nuts," he said. "I haven't been hurt yet. When I am, it might be a different tune."

"Maybe," she said. "Wait and hear how I sing."

He reached out and squeezed her thigh.

"Okay, Corny. You've been okay so far. Hang on to that piece, and we'll see what happens."

He reached for another cigarette, found the pack empty, cursed. He gestured toward a compartment, and she opened it and got him a fresh pack. She tore it open and lit him one.

"Thanks."

"Why're they staying out of range?"

"Maybe they're just going to pace us. I don't know."

Then the fogs began to lift. By the time Tanner had finished his cigarette, the visibility had improved greatly. He could make out the dark forms crouched atop their bikes, following, following, nothing more.

"If they just want to keep us company, then I don't care," he said. "Let them."

But there came more gunfire after a time, and he heard a tire go. He slowed but continued. He took careful aim and strafed them. Several fell.

More gunshots sounded from behind. Another tire blew, and he hit the brakes and skidded, turning about as he slowed. When he faced them, he shot his anchors, to hold him in place, and he discharged his rockets, one after another, at a level parallel to the road. He opened up with his guns and sprayed them as they veered off and approached him from the sides. Then he opened fire to the left. Then the right.

He emptied the right-hand guns, then switched back to the left. He launched the remaining grenades.

The gunfire died down, except for five sources—three to his left and two to his right—coming from somewhere within the trees that lined the road now. Broken bikes and bodies lay behind him, some still smoldering. The pavement was potted and cracked in many places.

He turned the car and proceeded ahead on six wheels.

"We're out of ammo, Corny," he told her.

"Well, we took an awful lot of them. . . ."

"Yeah."

As he drove on, he saw five bikes move onto the road. They stayed a good distance behind him, but they stayed.

He tried the radio, but there was no response. He hit the brakes and stopped, and the bikes stopped too, staying well to the rear.

"Well, at least they're scared of us. They think we still have teeth."

"We do," she said.

"Yeah, but not the ones they're thinking about."

"Better yet."

"Glad I met you," said Tanner. "I can use an optimist. There must be a pony, huh?"

She nodded, and he put it into gear and started forward.

The motorcycles moved ahead also, and they maintained a safe distance. Tanner watched them in the screens and cursed them as they followed.

After a while they drew nearer again. Tanner roared on for half an hour, and the remaining five edged closer and closer.

When they drew near enough, they began to fire, rifles resting on their handlebars.

Tanner heard several low ricochets, and then another tire went out.

He stopped once more and the bikes did too,

remaining just out of range of his flames. He cursed and ground ahead again. The car wobbled as he drove, listing to the left. A wrecked pickup truck stood smashed against a tree on his right, its hunched driver a skeleton, its windows smashed and tires missing. Half a sun now stood in the heavens, reaching after nine o'clock; fog-ghosts drifted before them, and the dark band in the sky undulated, and more rain fell from it, mixed with dust and small stones and bits of metal. Tanner said, "Good," as the pinging sounds began, and, "Hope it gets a lot worse," and his wish came true as the ground began to shake and the blue light began in the north. There came a booming within the roar, and there were several answering crashes as heaps of rubble appeared to his right. "Hope the next one falls right on our buddies back there," he said.

He saw an orange glow ahead and to his right. It had been there for several minutes, but he had not become conscious of it until just then.

"Volcano," she said when he indicated it. "It means we've got another sixty-five, seventy miles to go."

He could not tell whether any more shooting was occurring. The sounds coming from overhead and around him were sufficient to mask any gunfire, and the fall of gravel upon the car covered any ricocheting rounds. The five headlights to his rear maintained their pace.

"Why don't they give up?" he said. "They're taking a pretty bad beating."

"They're used to it," she replied, "and they're riding for blood, which makes a difference."

Tanner fetched the .357 Magnum from the door clip and passed it to her. "Hang on to this too," he said, and he found a box of ammo in the second compartment and, "Put these in your pocket," he added. He stuffed ammo for the .45 into his own jacket. He adjusted the hand grenades upon his belt.

Then the five headlights behind him suddenly became four, and the others slowed, grew smaller. "Accident, I hope," he remarked.

They sighted the mountain, a jag-topped cone bleeding fires upon the sky. They left the road and swung far to the left, upon a well-marked trail. It took twenty minutes to pass the mountain, and by then he sighted their pursuers once again—four lights to the rear, gaining slowly.

He came upon the road once more and hurried ahead across the shaking ground. The yellow lights moved through the heavens, and heavy, shapeless objects, some several feet across, crashed to the earth about them. The car was buffeted by winds, listed as they moved, would not proceed above forty miles an hour. The radio contained only static.

Tanner rounded a sharp curve, hit the brake, turned off his lights, pulled the pin from a hand grenade, and waited with his hand upon the door.

When the lights appeared in the screen, he flung the door wide, leaped down, and hurled the grenade back through the abrasive rain.

He was into the cab again before he heard the explosion, before the flash occurred upon his screen.

The girl laughed almost hysterically as the car moved ahead.

"You got 'em, Hell! You got 'em!" she cried.

Tanner took a drink from her flask, and she finished its final brown mouthful. He lit them cigarettes.

The road grew cracked, pitted, slippery. They topped a high rise and headed downhill. The fogs thickened as they descended.

Lights appeared before him, and he readied the flame. There were no hostilities, however, as he passed a truck headed in the other direction. Within the next half hour he passed two more.

There came more lightning, and fist-sized rocks began to fall. Tanner left the road and sought shelter within a grove of high trees. The sky grew completely black, losing even its blue aurora.

They waited for three hours, but the storm did not let up. One by one, the four view screens went dead, and the fifth showed only the blackness beneath the car. Tanner's last sight in the rearview screen was of a huge splintered tree with a broken, swaying branch that was about ready to fall off. There were several terrific crashes upon the hood, and the car shook with each. The roof above their heads was deeply dented in three places. The lights grew dim, then bright again. The radio would not produce even static anymore.

"I think we've had it," he said.

"Yeah."

"How far are we?"

"Maybe fifty miles away."

"There's still a chance, if we live through this."

"What chance?"

They reclined their seats and smoked and waited, and after a while the lights went out.

The storm continued all that day and into the night. They slept within the broken body of the car, and it sheltered them. When the storming ceased, Tanner opened the door and looked outside, closed it again.

"We'll wait till morning," he said, and she held his Hell-printed hand, and they slept.

Henry Soames, M.D., knew that he was losing. The bells kept telling him so. He covered the boy and nodded to Miss Akers, all in white.

"Dead," he said, "obviously. Have them type it up so I can sign it."

She nodded. "Cremation?" she said.

"Yes."

Then he moved on and regarded the girl. "Evvie?" he asked her.

"Yes?" from far away.

"How are you feeling?"

"Could I have a drink?"

"Sure. Here."

He poured her a glass of water, raised her, and held it to her lips. Soon he would contract it himself, he knew. It couldn't be otherwise. Too much exposure....

"Where's Fred?" she asked after she had drunk.

"Sleeping."

Then she closed her perspiration-ringed eyes, and he lowered her and moved on to another.

"How long has she got?" asked Miss Akers, all in white.

"A day or two," he replied.

"Then there's a chance, if the serum comes?"

"Yes. If the serum comes."

"You don't think it will?"

"No. It's too far, too much. The odds are too great."

"I think it will."

"Good," he said. "A true beliver." Then, "I'm sorry, Karen. I didn't mean that. I'm tired."

"I know. You haven't slept for two nights, have you?"

"I got a nap a little while ago."

"An hour doesn't mean much when the fatigue factor is so high."

"True. But I'm sorry."

"There's a chance," she said. "You may not think so, but my brother is a driver. He thinks the Alley can be run."

"Both ways? In time? I don't. It would take an awful lot of luck, and the best drivers they've got. And we don't really know if they still have the serum, even. I think this is it."

"Maybe."

He slapped his clipboard against his thigh.

"Why speculate?" he said. "That girl could be saved. Very easily. Just get me some Haffikine, and I can start treating her. Otherwise, we're just keeping score."

"I know. It'll come, though."

"I hope so."

He stopped to take a pulse.

"Okay."

They moved along the corridor, and she touched his arm.

"Don't hurt," she said, all in white.

"It's not a thing that can be helped. Nobody's to blame, but there's nothing that can be done."

"Room one-thirty-six is empty," she said.

He stood very still for a moment, then nodded.

She was right, and as they lay there he thought of the Alley and its ways, but did not say aloud what he felt.

"Soon," she told him. "Soon. Don't worry so much."

He stroked her shoulder.

"Do you remember the Three Days?" he asked.

"No."

"I do," he said. "We put people on the moon and Mars and Titan. We conquered space. We lost time. We had a United Nations. But what happened? Three lousy days, that's what, and everything went to hell. I was there when the rockets came down, Karen. I was there, and I listened to the radio until it stopped. They threw them all over the place. New York is a Hot Spot. So are most of the big cities. Maybe only the islands made it: the Caribbean, Hawaii, Japan, the Greek isles. They kept broadcasting for a long time, you know, after the others quit. Maybe there are still people alive in Japan and the Mediterranean. We know there are some in the Caribbean. I don't know. But I was there when it happened. It was terribly like this, the feeling of doom. I thought for a while recently that we might make it, though. I wonder if the people on Mars are still alive? Or Titan? Will they ever come back? I doubt they could. I think we're already dead, Karen. I think it's time for everybody to lie down and admit it. If we haven't screwed everything up, it's not because we didn't try. If the sky ever purges itself, I wonder if there'll be anyone left to know it? Maybe there will, on some island—or the West Coast. But I doubt it. If we make it, there'll be even more freaks than there are now. Man may cease being man, for God's sake!"

"We'll make it," she said. "People always screw up. But there are so many. Some will live."

"I hope you're right."

"Listen to the bells," she said. "Each one signifies death. They used to ring them on festival days too, signifying life. Some man will come, and he'll run the Alley, I think. But if he doesn't, we won't all die. The Three Days were bad. I know. I've heard about them. Don't give up, though, on that account."

"I can't help it. I feel—lost."

Then she touched him and said, "All you can do is what you're doing. The only other thing is how you feel about it. I don't remember the Three Days, but even that wasn't final. Remember that.

We're still here, come everything."

He kissed her then, and the room was dark and antiseptic around them. "You're the kind of people we need," he said, and she shook her head.

"I'm just a nurse. Why don't you sleep now? I'll make the rounds for you. You rest. Maybe tomorrow . . ."

"Yeah. Maybe tomorrow," he said. "I don't believe it, but thanks."

After a while she heard him snore, and she rose up from the bed. She departed Room 136, all in white, and made his rounds for him.

The bells shattered the air about her, for the clinic was near to three churches, but she made the rounds, taking pulses and temperatures, pouring water, smiling; and although she did not remember the Three Days, she knew that she lived in them still, each time that she entered a ward.

But she smiled, which was man's last weapon, perhaps.

In the morning, Tanner walked back through the mud and the fallen branches, the rocks and the dead fish, and he opened the rear compartment and unbolted the bikes. He fueled them and checked them out and wheeled them down the ramp.

He crawled into the back of the cab then and removed the rear seat. Beneath it, in the storage compartment, was the large aluminum chest that was his cargo. It was bolted shut. He lifted it, carried it out to his bike.

"That the stuff?"

He nodded and placed it on the ground.

"I don't know how the stuff is stored, if it's refrigerated in there or what," he said, "but it ain't too heavy that I might not be able to get it on the back of my bike. There's straps in the far-right compartment. Go get 'em and give me a hand—and get me my pardon out of the middle compartment. It's in a big cardboard envelope."

She returned with these things and helped him secure the container on the rear of his bike.

He wrapped extra straps around his left bicep, and they wheeled the machines to the road.

"We'll have to take it kind of slow," he said, and he slung the rifle over his right shoulder, drew on his gloves, and kicked his bike to life.

She did the same with hers, and they moved forward, side by side, along the highway.

After they had been riding for perhaps an hour, two cars passed them, heading west. In the rear seats of both there were children, who pressed their faces to the glass and watched them as they went by. The driver of the second car was in his shirt sleeves, and he wore a black shoulder holster.

The sky was pink, and there were three black lines that looked as if they could be worth worrying about. The sun was a rose-tinted silvery thing, and pale, but Tanner still had to raise his goggles against it.

The cargo was riding securely, and Tanner leaned into the dawn and thought about Boston. There was a light mist on the foot of every hill, and the air was cool and moist. Another car passed them. The road surface began to improve.

It was around noontime when he heard the first shot above the thunder of their engines. At first he thought it was a backfire, but it came again, and Corny cried out and swerved off the road and struck a boulder.

Tanner cut to the left, braking, as two more shots struck about him, and he leaned his bike against a tree and threw himself flat. A shot struck near his head, and he could tell the direction from which it had come. He crawled into a ditch and drew off his right glove. He could see his girl lying where she had fallen, and there was blood on her breast. She did not move.

He raised the 30.06 and fired.

The shot was returned, and he moved to his left.

It had come from a hill about two hundred feet away, and he thought he saw the rifle's barrel.

He aimed at it and fired again.

The shot was returned, and he wormed his way farther left. He crawled perhaps fifteen feet, until he reached a pile of rubble he could crouch behind. Then he pulled the pin on a grenade, stood, and hurled it.

He threw himself flat as another shot rang out, and he took another grenade into his hand.

There was a roar and a rumble and a mighty flash, and the junk fell about him as he leaped to his feet and threw the second one, taking better aim this time.

After the second explosion, he ran forward

with his rifle in his hands, but it wasn't necessary.

He found only a few small pieces of the man, and none at all of his rifle.

He returned to Cornelia.

She wasn't breathing, and her heart had stopped beating, and he knew what that meant.

He carried her back to the ditch in which he had lain, and he made it deeper by digging, using his hands.

He laid her down in it, and he covered her with the dirt. Then he wheeled her machine over, set the kickstand, and stood it upon the grave. With his knife he scratched on the fender: *Her name was Cornelia and I don't know how old she was or where she came from or what her last name was but she was Hell Tanner's girl and I love her.* Then he went back to his own machine, started it, and drove ahead. Boston was maybe thirty miles away.

● ● ●

Setting without plot or characters. Put a frame around it if you would, and call it what you would, if you would: Chaos, Creation, Nightmare of the Periodic Table or _____ [fill in your own].

It looks like this: There are thousands of pillars such as those the gallant airman Mermoz saw when first he crossed the South Atlantic in a hydroplane and negotiated that region called the Black Hole off the coast of Africa—giant pillars in which rumbles the upsurge of the sea and the land—the tails of tornadoes—as Saint-Exupéry described them, "rising as a wall is built"—and they sway at first, swelling at their tops and stand then as immobile as architecture, supporting the arch of the mighty winds that circle the world unceasing, feeding those winds with the harvest of the waters and the lands, limned, etched, sketched, sometimes charcoaled by the lightnings that flicker first, then pulse, like pinwheels or spiders with too many legs or Chinese characters that trace, chase, rewrite themselves in baleful red, lavish yellow, cold blue, blinding white, and occasional green and mystic violet, according to the changing medium through which they move, all in the space of the eyeball's twitching, if you're there to see, and may you never, how the sky takes up within itself the land and the water, separated since the days of creation, turns them to plasma, pinches them into rivers that race darkly through its dotted aerography, disperses them into clouds like nebulae, harasses them from sunset to sunrise and on into the night, drowns stars in their depths, cancels out the moon or colors it any, throttles the sun or dyes it, blackens the dome of the world or Easter-eggs it, moving at great heights or lesser ones, shifting, always shifting, juggling a billion particles of solids, liquids, and gases, through orbits that only such winds may maintain for a time, sometimes shattering, or being shattered against the tops of mountains, high trees, tall buildings, sometimes bellying to devastate the flat land itself and deck it with smashings, color it ruined, plowed, fertilized, dropping also rains, of stone, wood, the dead of the sea and the land, masonry, metal, sand, fire, fabric, glass, coral, and water sometimes, too, as it disciplines the earth and the seas which perhaps abused it too much, too long, by bringing forth those who respected no pacts between the basic elements, who smudged the heavens with a million pollutants and fear, filling the bottle above the air with the radioactivity of five hundred prematurely detonated warheads, aborted by a radiation level already raised to the point where it broke them apart with spontaneous chain reactions, troubling its still blue on those three days when the pacts were broken, so that within its still heights the clouds were torn apart and swept away before the wailing it raised up to protest this final too familiar familiarity, so that perhaps the word it cries is "Rape!" or maybe "Help!" or "God!" even, and the fact that it cries at all may hold hope and the promise of an eventual purging, of the land and the sea as well as the air, and then again, perhaps not, for it could equally be the banshee wail of doom near at hand that rises from its round throat that swalloweth and spitteth forth again; and as it surges by, perhaps it takes fire from the hot spots where the cobalt bombs fell and, of course, perhaps not also; for these, with their own pulses of death, are of the earth, if anything, and that which they do may not offend the low-stooping heavens or provoke them to greater movement; but consider for a moment the thousand pillars of the sky, plus many, which force the premonition that the world is a forbidden place for man to enter: standing as they do to feed the circling winds, these things may even be worshiped one day, if they persist and prospective worshipers do likewise, for they rise like angels from the dust or the green tiles of the sea, shrug their unhuman shoulders and soar up into the place where no man may go, and then like the communion of saints link that which is above with that which is below, effecting a transference of essence before they lapse into quietude, winding or unwinding themselves like barbers' poles or springs; and of all these things which the sky gives and takes back again, altered, to be sure, there is none which breaks the heart more than life, if you're there to see, and may you never, how brightness is traded for darkness and undergoes a sea-change where once there was no sea, but sunlight and blue and cirrus and piles of cumulus, as a city, a house, a dog, a man ascends into the heavens, is transfigured, returns again as dross, the straw and mud of the primal ooze that drips like spittle from the lips that were blue, perhaps to start again all single-celled and still, but probably not, for the ways of the winds seem not the ways of man or of life, but rather, as the gallant Mermoz must have noted that day, that night, despite their nearness they are distant.

It is this, more than anything else in the entire world, that demands regard.

A setting, nothing more—no plot, no characters.

Because of this nearness and this distance.

Put a frame around it if you would, and call it what you would, if you would.

But the winds will scream with the seven voices of judgment, if you're there to hear them, and may you never, and it just doesn't seem that any name will fit.

He drove along, and after a time he heard the sound of another bike. A Harley cut onto the road from the dirt path to his left, and he couldn't try running away from it because he couldn't speed with the load he bore. So he allowed himself to be paced.

After a while the rider of the other bike—a tall, thin man with a flaming beard—drew up alongside him, to the left. He smiled and raised his right hand and let it fall and then gestured with his head.

Tanner braked and came to a halt. Redbeard was right beside him when he did. He said, "Where you going, man?"

"Boston."

"What you got in the box?"

"Like, drugs."

"What kind?" and the man's eyebrows arched and the smile came again onto his lips.

"For the plague they got going there."

"Oh. I thought you meant the other kind."

"Sorry."

The man held a pistol in his right hand, and he said, "Get off your bike."

Tanner did this, and the man raised his left hand, and another man came forward from the brush at the side of the road. "Wheel this guy's bike about two hundred yards up the highway," he said, "and park it in the middle. Then take your place."

"What's the bit?" Tanner asked.

The man ignored the question. "Who are you?" he asked.

"Hell's the name," he replied. "Hell Tanner."

"Go to hell."

Tanner shrugged.

"You ain't Hell Tanner."

Tanner drew off his right glove and extended his fist.

"There's my name."

"I don't believe it," said the man after he had studied the tattoo.

Hell shrugged. "Have it your way, citizen."

"Shut up!" and he raised his left hand once more, now that the other man had parked the machine on the road and returned to a place somewhere within the trees to the right.

In response to his gesture, there was movement within the brush.

Bikes were pushed forward by their riders, and they lined the road, twenty or thirty on either side.

"There you are," said the man. "My name's Big Brother."

"Glad to meet you."

"You know what you're going to do, mister?"

"I can guess."

"You're going to walk up to your bike and claim it."

Tanner smiled. "How hard's that going to be?"

"No trouble at all. Just start walking. Give me your rifle first, though."

Big Brother raised his hand again, and one by one the engines came to life.

"Okay," he said. "Now."

"You think I'm crazy, man?"

"No. Start walking. Your rifle..."

Tanner unslung it, and he continued the arc. He caught Big Brother beneath his red beard with its butt, and he felt a bullet go into his side. Then he dropped the weapon and hauled forth a grenade, pulled the pin, and tossed it amid the left side of the gauntlet. Before it exploded, he'd pulled the pin on another and thrown it to his right. By then, though, vehicles were moving forward, heading toward him.

He fell upon the rifle and shouldered it in a prone firing position. As he did this, the first explosion occurred. He was firing before the second one went off.

He dropped three of them, then got to his feet and scrambled, firing from the hip.

He made it behind Big Brother's fallen bike and fired from there. Big Brother was still fallen, too. When the rifle was empty, he didn't have time to reload. He fired the .45 four times before a tire chain brought him down.

He awoke to the roaring of the engines. They were circling him. When he got to his feet, a handlebar knocked him down again.

Two bikes were moving about him, and there

were many dead people upon the road.

He struggled to rise again, was knocked off his feet.

Big Brother rode one of the bikes, and a guy he hadn't seen rode the other.

He crawled to the right, and there was pain in his fingertips as tires passed over them.

But he saw a rock and waited till a driver was near. Then he stood again and threw himself upon the man as he passed, the rock he had seized rising and falling, once, in his right hand. He was carried along as this occurred, and as he fell he felt the second bike strike him.

There were terrible pains in his side, and his body felt broken, but he reached out even as this occurred and caught hold of a strut on the side of the bike, and was dragged along by it.

Before he had been dragged ten feet, he had drawn his SS dagger from his boot. He struck upward and felt a thin metal wall give way. Then his hands came loose, and he fell, and he smelled the gasoline. His hand dived into his jacket pocket and came out with the Zippo.

He had struck the tank on the side of Big Brother's bike, and it jetted forth its contents on the road. Thirty feet ahead, Big Brother was turning.

Tanner held the lighter, the lighter with the raised skull of enamel, wings at its back. His thumb spun the wheel, and the sparks leaped forth, then the flame. He tossed it into the stream of gasoline that lay before him, and the flames raced away, tracing a blazing trail upon the concrete.

Big Brother had turned and was bearing down upon him when he saw what had happened. His eyes widened, and his red-framed smile went away.

He tried to leap off his bike, but it was too late.

The exploding gas tank caught him, and he went down with a piece of metal in his head and other pieces elsewhere.

Flames splashed over Tanner, and he beat at them feebly with his hands.

He raised his head above the blazing carnage and let it fall again. He was bloody and weak and so very tired. He saw his own machine, standing still undamaged on the road ahead.

He began crawling toward it.

When he reached it, he threw himself across the saddle and lay there for perhaps ten minutes. He vomited twice, and his pains became a steady pulsing.

After perhaps an hour he mounted the bike and brought it to life.

He rode for half a mile, and then the dizziness and the fatigue hit him.

He pulled off to the side of the road and concealed his bike as best he could. Then he lay down upon the bare earth and slept.

Within the theater Agony on the stage of Delirium in the heat-lightning lit landscape of

Night and Dream there go upon the boards the memories that never were, compounded of that which was and that which is not, that which is and that which can never be, informed with fleeting or lingering passions, sexless or sexful, profound or absurd, seldom remembered, sometimes coherent, beautiful, ugly, or mundane upon experience, generally inane in reflection, strangely sad or happy, colorfully dark or darkly light, and this is about all that can be said of them, save that the spark which ignites them, too, is unknown.

A man in black moves along a broken roadway beneath a dimly glowing sky.

I am Father Dearth, a priest out of Albany, he seems to say, making my pilgrimage to the cathedral in Boston, going down to Boston to pray for the salvation of man. Over the mountains, down the Alley, by a foam-flecked stream, past the blazing mountain and over the swaying bridges, heavily my footfall rings. In this wood beside the road, there will I await the dawn, there where the dew lies thick.

There comes a sound, as of the steady rumble of an engine, but it neither rises nor diminishes in volume. Then to it is added the sound as of one striking upon a fender with a stone at five-second intervals. This continues.

Another approaches the wood, dressed all in gray and wearing a red mask with concentric circles about the eyeholes, a thin line for a mouth, sunken cheeks, and three dark V's in the center of the forehead.

I would speak to you, priest, he seems to say, coming to stand beside the other.

What is it you would say?

There is a man for whom I would beg you pray.

This is my part. For whom shall I pray?

There is no need to know his name. He lies far from here. He is buried in another land.

How can I pray for him if I do not know his name?

Pray, nevertheless. All creatures shall be profited without distinction.

This I cannot do.

And between the steady beats and within the rumble, the measured words are made, saying, Pray, though the heart that prays marks with no name the prayer, yet he that takes it is its owner.

Then come with me to my home and pass the night there, priest.

He raises a branch, and there is a doorway.

What is this place? A shrine, of sorts? It seems like the inside of a car, only much larger.

It is.

The one in the mask seats himself before the wheel and places his hands upon it. He stares forward then and does not move.

Who are you?

It does not matter. I drive.

Where? Why? What is the reason for this?

You must know that when I put forth upon my mission I did not want to die. I was afraid, but I drove. Past, over, through all things that stood in my way I drove, and the bolts out of the heavens fell about me, driving, and the sleep piled up behind my eyes after my comrade died, and I fought it with drugs and my will, knowing as I drove that the invisible fires of radiation burned my body, coming from beyond my damaged shield. Driving, I became a part of the car, and it of me, so that we were one with our mission. I am wounded again and again now with this fire, and my head grows more heavy.

Slowly, he lowers his head to the wheel and rests it there, unmoving.

Swiftly, swiftly coming and swiftly going, coming and going. One night, two nights, three nights. I carved my tracks upon the Alley, my eyes dazzled and a madness possessing me. My wounds are upon me, and there is no end to the road I drive.

He raises his head once more.

They kill me, the monsters in the land and the sky. They kill me. Driving, driving, I reach my destination, deliver my message, sicken, and die.

But I must have done, or dawn will find me talking still. Go to your rest through yonder door.

He rises and departs the car, and the priest passes through the doorway, to stand in the grove once more, for the car has vanished, though the sound of the engine continues undiminished and the steady beat does not wane.

I have seen strange things. I cannot sleep. I will pray.

The priest bows his head and stands motionless for a time.

The one mask appears once more, with a bandage about his head.

The winds are rising, he seems to say, the clouds shift, and the night is dark. A wild wind combs the wood beneath this hill. The branches heave. The moon does not rise till dawn, and then she will be invisible. There is no quietness, nor is there rest.

Say your name.

The man raises one hand to his mask and covers it over. He turns away his head.

Brady. Give me rest.

Then the mask and the bandage drop to the ground, and the gray garment collapses upon them, as day begins faintly in the east.

The words are made within the rumble and the beats: He was wounded, until the strength of his spirit weakened, like the dew that even now fades.

A cock is crowing, and a whiteness begins in the sky. He has hidden under the shadow of the trees; under the shadow of the trees has he hidden himself.

The dream is vanished now; where to, too, is not known.

When he awoke, he felt dried blood upon his side. His left hand ached and was swollen. All four fingers felt stiff, and it hurt to try to bend them. His head throbbed, and there was a taste of gasoline within his mouth. He was too sore to move for a long while. His beard had been singed, and his right eye was swollen almost shut.

"Corny..." he said; then, "Damn!"

Everything came back, like the contents of a powerful dream suddenly spilled into his consciousness.

He began to shiver, and there were mists all around him. It was very dark, and his legs were cold; the dampness had soaked completely through his denims.

In the distance, he heard a vehicle pass. It sounded like a car.

He managed to roll over, and he rested his head on his forearm. It seemed to be night, but it could be a black day.

As he lay there, his mind went back to his prison cell. It seemed almost a haven now; and he thought of his brother, Denny, who must also be hurting at this moment. He wondered if he had any cracked ribs himself. It felt like it. And he thought of the monsters of the southwest, and of dark-eyed Greg, who had tried to chicken out. Was he still living? His mind circled back to L.A. and the old Coast, gone, gone forever now, after the Big Raid. Then Corny walked past him, blood upon her breasts, and he chewed his beard and held his eyes shut very tight. They might have made it together in Boston. How far, now?

He got to his knees and crawled until he felt something high and solid. A tree. He sat with his back to it, and his hand sought the crumpled cigarette pack within his jacket. He drew one forth, smoothed it, then remembered that his lighter lay somewhere back on the highway. He sought through his pockets and found a damp matchbook. The third one lit. The chill went out of his bones as he smoked, and a wave of fever swept over him. He coughed as he was unbuttoning his collar, and it seemed that he tasted blood.

His weapons were gone, save for the lump of a single grenade at his belt.

Above him, in the darkness, he heard the roaring. After six puffs, the cigarette slipped from his fingers and sizzled out upon the damp mold. His head fell forward, and there was darkness within.

There might have been a storm. He didn't remember. When he awoke, he was lying on his right side, the tree to his back. A pink afternoon sun shone down upon him, and the mists were blown away. From somewhere he heard the sound of a bird. He managed a curse, then realized how dry his throat was. He was suddenly burned with a terrible thirst.

There was a clear puddle about thirty feet away. He crawled to it and drank his fill. It grew muddy as he did so.

Then he crawled to where his bike lay hidden, and stood beside it. He managed to seat himself upon it, and his hands shook as he lit a cigarette.

It must have taken him an hour to reach the roadway, and he was panting heavily by then. His watch had been broken, so he didn't know the hour. The sun was already lowering at his back when he started out. The winds whipped about him, insulating his consciousness within their burning flow. His cargo rode securely behind him. He had visions of someone opening it and finding a batch of broken bottles. He laughed and cursed, alternately.

Several cars passed him, heading in the other direction. He had not seen any heading toward the city. The road was in good condition, and he began to pass buildings that seemed in a good state of repair, though deserted. He did not stop. This time he determined not to stop for anything, unless he was stopped.

The sun fell farther, and the sky dimmed before him. There were two black lines swaying in the heavens. Then he passed a sign that told him he had eighteen miles farther to go. Ten minutes later he switched on his light.

Then he topped a hill and slowed before he began its descent.

There were lights below him and in the distance.

As he rushed forward, the winds brought to him the sound of a single bell, tolling over and over within the gathering dark. He sniffed a remembered thing upon the air: it was the salt tang of the sea.

The sun was hidden behind the hill as he descended, and he rode within the endless shadow. A single star appeared on the far horizon, between the two black belts.

Now there were lights within shadows that he passed, and the buildings moved closer together. He leaned heavily on the handlebars, and the muscles of his shoulders smoldered beneath his jacket. He wished that he had a crash helmet, for he felt increasingly unsteady.

He must be almost there. Where would he head, once he hit the city proper? They had not told him that.

He shook his head to clear it.

The street he drove along was deserted. There were no traffic sounds that he could hear. He blew his horn, and its echoes rolled back upon him.

There was a light on in the building to his left.

He pulled to a stop, crossed the sidewalk, and banged on the door. There was no response from within. He tried the door and found it locked. A telephone would mean he could end his trip right there.

What if they were all dead inside? The thought occurred to him that just about everybody could be dead by now. He decided to break in. He returned to his bike for a screwdriver, then went to work on the door.

He heard the gunshot and the sound of the engine at approximately the same time.

He turned around quickly, his back against the door, the hand grenade in his gloved right fist.

"Hold it!" called out a loudspeaker on the side of the black car that approached. "That shot was a warning! The next one won't be!"

Tanner raised his hands to a level with his ears, his right one turned to conceal the grenade. He stepped forward to the curb beside his bike when the car drew up.

There were two officers in the car, and the one on the passenger side held a .38 pointed at Tanner's middle.

"You're under arrest," he said. "Looting."

Tanner nodded as the man stepped out of the car. The driver came around the front of the vehicle, a pair of handcuffs in his hand.

"Looting," the man with the gun repeated. "You'll pull a real stiff sentence."

"Stick your hands out here, boy," said the second cop, and Tanner handed him the grenade pin.

The man stared at it dumbly for several seconds; then his eyes shot to Tanner's right hand.

"God! He's got a bomb!" said the man with the gun.

Tanner smiled, then, "Shut up and listen!" he said. "Or else shoot me and we'll all go together when we go. I was trying to get to a telephone. That case on the back of my bike is full of Haffikine antiserum. I brought it from L.A."

"You didn't run the Alley on that bike!"

"No, I didn't. My car is dead somewhere between here and Albany, and so are a lot of folks who tried to stop me. Now, you better take that medicine and get it where it's supposed to go in a hurry."

"You on the level, mister?"

"My hand is getting very tired. I am not in good shape." Tanner leaned on his bike. "Here."

He pulled his pardon out of his jacket and handed it to the officer with the handcuffs.

"That's my pardon," he said. "It's dated just last week, and you can see it was made out in California."

The officer took the envelope and opened it. He withdrew the paper and studied it. "Looks real," he said. "So Brady made it through. . . ."

"He's dead," Tanner said. "Look, I'm hurtin'. Do something!"

"My God! Hold it tight! Get in the car and sit down! It'll just take a minute to get the case off, and we'll roll. We'll drive to the river, and you can throw it in. Squeeze real hard!"

They unfastened the case and put it in the back of the car. They rolled down the right-front window, and Tanner sat next to it with his arm on the outside.

The siren screamed, and the pain crept up Tanner's arm to his shoulder. It would be very easy to let go.

"Where do you keep your river?" he asked.

"Just a little farther. We'll be there in no time."

"Hurry," Tanner said.

"That's the bridge up ahead. We'll ride out onto it, and you throw it off—as far out as you can."

"Man, I'm tired! I'm not sure I can make it. . . ."

"Hurry, Jerry!"

"I am, damn it! We ain't got wings!"

"I feel kind of dizzy, too. . . ."

They tore out onto the bridge, and the tires screeched as they halted. Tanner opened the door slowly. The driver's had already slammed shut.

He staggered, and they helped him to the

railing. He sagged against it when they released him.

"I don't think I—"

Then he straightened, drew back his arm, and hurled the grenade far out over the waters.

He grinned, and the explosion followed, far beneath them, and for a time the waters were troubled.

The two officers sighed, and Tanner chuckled.

"I'm really okay," he said. "I just faked it to bug you."

"Why you—!"

Then he collapsed, and they saw the pallor of his face within the beams of their lights.

The following spring, on the day of its unveiling in Boston Common, when it was discovered that someone had scrawled obscene words on the statue of Hell Tanner, no one thought to ask the logical candidate why he had done it, and the next day it was too late, because he had cut out without leaving a forwarding address. Several cars were reported stolen that day, and one was never seen again in Boston.

So they reveiled his statue, bigger than life, astride a great bronze Harley, and they cleaned him up for hoped-for posterity. But coming upon the Common, the winds still break about him, and the heavens still throw garbage.